BATTLES
IN THE DESERT
& OTHER
STORIES

By José Emilio Pacheco

BATTLES IN THE DESERT & OTHER STORIES
Translated by Katherine Silver

SELECTED POEMS
Edited by George McWhirter

José Emilio Pacheco

BATTLES IN THE DESERT & OTHER STORIES

Translated by Katherine Silver

A NEW DIRECTIONS BOOK

The translated works of José Emilio Pacheco included in this collection were published, in the original Spanish, in the following volumes: *El viento distante* (Mexico City: Ediciones Era, S. A., 1963); *El principio del placer* (Mexico City: Editorial Joaquín Mortiz, S. A., 1972); *Las batallas en el desierto* (Mexico City: Ediciones Era, S. A., 1981).

Manufactured in the United States of America
First published clothbound and as New Directions Paperback 637 in 1987
Published simultaneously in Canada by Penguin Books Canada Ltd.

Library of Congress Cataloging-in-Publication Data

Pacheco, José Emilio.
    Battles in the desert & other stories.

    Translated from Spanish.
    1. Pacheco, José Emilio—Translations, English.
I. Title.
PQ7298.26.A25A27   1987   863   86-28596
ISBN 0-8112-1019-7
ISBN 0-8112-1020-0 (pbk.)
ISBN-13: 978-0-811-21020-1

Second Printing

New Directions Books are published for James Laughlin
by New Directions Publishing Corporation,
80 Eighth Avenue, New York 10011

CONTENTS

THE PLEASURE PRINCIPLE

To Arturo Ripstein

You aren't going to believe it, you'll just say I'm an idiot, but when I was younger I used to dream about being able to fly, being invisible, and watching movies at home. They used to tell me: Wait until we have television. It's just like having your very own little movie theater in your room. Now that I'm grown up, I can laugh at all that. But of course now we have television, and I know that nobody can fly except in an airplane and that the potion to make you invisible hasn't been discovered yet.

I remember the very first time. They put a television set in the Regalos Nietos Gift Shop window and there were crowds of people on the corner of Juárez and Letrán trying to get a glimpse of the little figures. They only showed documentaries: hunting dogs, skiers, Hawaiian beaches, polar bears, supersonic airplanes.

Who am I talking to anyway? I guess no one will ever read this diary. I got it as a Christmas present, and I haven't wanted to write in it at all. Keeping a diary is for girls, I think, and I've even teased my sister because she keeps one and writes all kinds of corny stuff in it: "Dear Diary, today I waited all day for Gabriel to call but he never did," and things like that. And it's a very short step from here to little perfumed envelopes, and the guys at school would laugh their heads off if they knew I was going in for these kinds of sissy things.

Our teacher, Mr. Castañeda, suggested that we keep a diary. That's why I even agreed to accept this little green notebook. At least it doesn't suck up all the ink like the ones we have at school. According to Castañeda, a diary teaches us how to think more

3

clearly because when we write, we put things in order, and then as
time passes it's interesting to see what we were once like, what we
did, what we thought about, how much we've changed.

By the way, he gave me an "A" on my composition about the
tree, and he had a poem I wrote for Mother's Day published in the
high-school newspaper. Nobody in the class is better than me in
composition and dictation. I make mistakes but I have the best
spelling and punctuation. I'm also good at history, civics, and English, but I'm a dope when it comes to physics, math, and drawing.
I don't think there's anybody else in my whole class who has read
all—well, almost all—of *The Treasury of Youth*, and all of Salgari
and a lot of Jules Verne's and Dumas's novels. I would read more
but Aceves told us we shouldn't read too much because it ruins your
eyesight and makes you weak-willed (?) Who can figure these
teachers out? One says one thing and the other says exactly the opposite.

It's funny to watch how the letters come together in little groups
and things appear that you never thought of saying. I now promise
to write down everything that happens to me. I would be very embarrassed if anybody saw this notebook. I'm going to hide it away
among my father's papers. No one will find it there (I hope).

෫෴

I haven't written here for a few months. From now on I'll try to
write every day or at least once a week. My silence can be explained
by the fact that we moved to Veracruz because my father was put in
charge of that military zone. I'm still not used to the heat, I'm not
sleeping very well, and to tell you the truth, school has been really
hard for me. I don't have any friends in my class, and my friends in
Mexico City don't write. The hardest thing was saying good-bye to
Marta. I hope she keeps her promise and talks her family into bringing her here for vacation. The house we rented isn't very big, but

it's right on the Malecón and it has a garden where I read and study when the sun isn't too hot. I love Veracruz. The only bad part about it (besides the heat) is that there are very few movie theaters and they don't have television yet.

I swim much better now and I've already learned how to drive. Durán, my father's new assistant, taught me how. And another thing: Every week there will be a wrestling match at the Díaz Mirón Movie Theater. I'll get permission to go if my grades improve.

Today I met Ana Luisa, a friend of my sisters', the daughter of the woman who makes their clothes. She lives right around the corner and works in The Yardage Paradise. I was very shy. Then I tried to seem very sure of myself and ended up saying a lot of stupid things.

After school, I stayed downtown and waited until Ana Luisa got off work. I walked down another block and got on her streetcar, the Villa del Mar por Bravo. It didn't turn out to be such a good move because she was with her friends from the store. I couldn't bring myself to go up to her, but I said, "Hi," and she was very friendly. What's going to happen? Mystery.

Quarter exams. They flunked me in chemistry and trigonometry. Luckily my mother agreed to sign the report card and not say anything to my father.

Yesterday, in Independencia, Pablo introduced me to a boy with glasses. Then he said, "You see? That guy went out with that girl you like." He didn't go into details and I didn't dare ask.

૩๑

I drove from Villa del Mar to Mocambo. Durán says I'm pretty good. He's a cool guy even though he's twenty-five years old. A cop stopped us and said it was because he thought I looked too young. Durán let him go right ahead and ask us for the license and learner's permit and threaten to throw us into the clink. Then Durán told him who the car belonged to and who I was and the problem was solved without having to pay him a cent.

૩๑

No sign of Ana Luisa for days. Seems like she had to go to Xalapa with her family. I keep going by her house but it's always closed up.

૩๑

I went to the movies with Durán. His girlfriend met us there. I liked her. She's nice. She's pretty even though she is a little fat and has some gold teeth. Her name is Candelaria and she works in Los Portales Pharmacy. We took her home and on our way back I told Durán about Ana Luisa. He said, "You should have told me sooner. I'm going to help you out. The four of us can go out together."

૩๑

I haven't written because nothing important has happened. Ana Luisa still hasn't come back. How could I have fallen in love with her when I don't even know her?

૩๑

Candelaria and Durán invited me to go out for ice cream. She asked me about Ana Luisa. Durán told her the whole story and then some. And now what?

ॐ

Something incredible happened to me today on my way home from school: I saw a dead person for the first time. Of course I'd seen pictures in *La Tarde,* but it's not the same at all, no way. There were a lot of people around and the ambulance hadn't arrived yet. Someone had covered his face with a pillowcase. Then some children pulled it off and I was horrified when I saw the gash in his chest, his mouth, and his open eyes. Worst of all was the blood that ran through the streets. Real thick, it was disgusting. The murder weapon was one of those tools they use to open coconuts. They're really more like double-edged knives with a wedge right down the middle that's used to gouge out the fruit. The victim was a longshoreman or a fisherman, I'm not quite sure. He had eight children and was killed by the lover of the woman who sells tamales in the alleyway out of jealousy. The murderer escaped. I hope they catch him. They say he was very drunk. The strangest thing about it is to think that people would kill each other for such an ugly, old woman. I thought only young people fell in love. And no matter what I do, I can't stop thinking about the body, that gruesome wound, the blood splattered all over, even on the walls. I don't know how my father did it during the Revolution, even though he told me that after a while you get used to seeing dead bodies.

ॐ

She's back. She came over to the house. I said, "Hi," but I didn't know what else to say to her. Then she went out with my sisters. How can I approach her?

8   José Emilio Pacheco

ह✍

On Sunday they're going to go to the movies and maybe afterward
to the Zócalo. I think I'll just show up there. Maricarmen asked me
if I liked Ana Luisa. And, like a coward, I said, "Are you kidding?
There are lots of girls a hundred times prettier than her."

ह✍

I went to the Zócalo at six-thirty. I saw Pablo and some other guys
from school, and I hung around with them. A while later Ana Luisa
and my sisters arrived. I invited them to have ice cream at the
Yucatán. We talked about movies and about Veracruz. Ana Luisa
wants to live in Mexico City. Durán came by in the big car, and we
took her home. Right after she got out, Nena and Maricarmen
started making fun of me. Sometimes I really hate my sisters. The
worst part was when Maricarmen said, "Don't get any smart ideas,
kiddo, because Ana Luisa already has a boyfriend, he's just not
around right now."

ह✍

After thinking it over for a long time, I decided to wait for Ana
Luisa at the streetcar stop in the afternoon. When she got out with
her friends, I greeted her and handed her a little piece of paper:

Ana Luisa:
   *I'm madly in love with you. I must talk to you alone. Tomorrow
I will come meet you just like today. Please give me your answer on
a piece of paper as I have done. Tell me when and where we can
meet or, if you'd rather, that you just want me to leave you alone.*
                                                              Jorge

Afterward I thought I blew it with that last sentence, but it was already too late. I have no idea what her answer will be. She'll probably tell me to go to hell.

ह•

I was restless all day, thinking about what Ana Luisa would say. But it turned out to be very different from what I had expected:

Jorge, I cant understand how your in love with me so lets talk. Well meet on sunday at noon at the chairs in villadelmar

Ana Luisa

ह•

Durán: "See what I mean? I told you it would be a cinch. Now listen to my advice and don't go blow it on Sunday."

Maricarmen: "What's the matter with you? Why are you so happy?"

The worst thing is that I didn't study at all.

ह•

I got there fifteen minutes early. I rented a chair and began reading one of Nena's books, *Philosophical Digest,* just so that Ana Luisa would see me with it. I couldn't concentrate at all. I was a nervous wreck. The clock struck twelve and no Ana Luisa. Then twelve-thirty and still nothing. I thought she wasn't going to show up. Just when I had finally talked myself into leaving, she appeared.

"Sorry. I couldn't get away."

"Get away? From whom?"

"What do you mean, who from? From my mother."

"Did you get my note?"

"Of course. And I answered it. That's why we're here."

"Oh, yeah, you're right. What an idiot I am . . . So, what do you think?"

"About what?"

"About what I said to you."

"Well, I don't know."

"What do you mean?"

"Give me some time. Let me think about it."

"You've already had plenty of time. Make up your mind."

"But like I told you, I don't hardly know you."

"I don't know you either and you see . . ."

"What?"

". . . I'm in love with you."

I turned bright red. I thought Ana Luisa was going to laugh. But she didn't say anything. She just smiled and took my hand. We walked silently along the Malecón toward the Fraccionamiento Reforma. I was happy even though I was a little worried that someone from home would see us. Suddenly Ana Luisa spoke. "Well, I guess I should admit that I like you pretty much too."

I didn't know what to say.

"But there's one problem."

"What's that?"

"You're younger than me."

"No, I'm not (I think) and even if I were, it wouldn't matter."

"Really?"

"Of course not."

I'd love to write down everything that happened today. But Maricarmen is wandering around, and it would be a disaster if she saw me writing. I'm going to hide this book away on the very top shelf of the closet. I'm very happy and everything turned out a thousand times better than I'd ever expected.

ᢒᕀ

For a whole week we've been meeting on the Malecón in the evenings. I haven't written anything because I'm afraid someone will read it (my sisters are gossips and they'll blab everything), but I feel like if I stop writing altogether nothing of anything that's happening now will remain. I don't even have a picture of Ana Luisa.

She doesn't want to give me one because she says that if they find it they'll tell her mother and

ۮ

Yesterday I had to stop because my father walked in. I told him I was doing my history homework and he believed me. He seems very nervous. In the southern part of the state there are problems with peasants who refuse to vacate some land the government wants in order to build another dam for the hydroelectric project. If things don't sort themselves out he's going to have to go there in person. I was talking about it with my mother today. She said that since the army is an army of the people it shouldn't shoot at the people. I don't know very much about my father; we almost never talk; but one time he told me that he used to be very poor and had gotten involved in the Revolution about a million years ago when he was around my age.

ۮ

A horrible day. Ana Luisa went to Xalapa again. She promised to write to me at Durán's girlfriend's house. At school, things are going from bad to worse. And to think that in elementary school I was one of the best students. . . .

ۮ

Durán took me out on the highway to practice. I drove from Mocambo to Boca del Río. Candelaria came with us and she promised me that as soon as Ana Luisa got back she would ask her mother for permission to go out *with her* and then the four of us could go out together.

ۮ

Candelaria called me and said she had received a letter from Ana Luisa and she would give it to Durán to give to me. I told her I would rather stop by and pick it up myself. But it's Sunday and I couldn't think of any excuse for leaving the house and so I have had to sit around all day dying of anxiety.

ॐ

Dear Jorge, Sorry I didnt rite you but I havent had any time and Ive had tons of problems and I dont have a second alone, just imagine that rite when we arrived my ant told my dad everything about me going out with you and who nows what else she told him. When she left my dad caled me in and told me what she told him and I told him it wasnt true that we went out but with your sisters and dont you think for a minute he beleved me.

Jorge the days seem like years without seeing you I always think about you at nite I go to sleep thinking about you I want you always by my side but theres no way what can we do???

Jorge hurry up and rite, send it to general delivery to LUISA BERROCAL, theyll give me the letter cos ive got id with that name.

Well so long Jorge. Im sending you lots a kisses and I love you and wont forget you

Ana Luisa

ॐ

Now that I've copied the letter down word for word, I'll try writing a rough draft of my answer right here:

My love (no, better:) *Dear Ana Luisa* (no, that sounds too cold) *My beloved and unforgettable Ana Luisa* (too corny) *My dear* (not strong enough) *My dearest Ana Luisa* (that's okay, I guess):

You can't imagine the great joy your long-awaited letter gave me (doesn't sound great but anyways, here goes). *Nor can you imagine how much I miss you and how much I need to see you. Now I know for certain that I am deeply in love with you.*

*Even so, I must be truthful and tell you that there were three
very strange things in your letter:*

*First: I thought that the woman you live with is your mother and
now you say that she's your aunt. (On top of that, you never told
me your father was in Xalapa.)*

*Second: Why can't you come back? Why do you have to go to
Xalapa all the time? I am very concerned about all these things and
I beg you to please clear things up.*

*Third: I'm sending this to General Delivery and to the name you
mentioned, but to tell you the truth, I don't understand how you
can have identification under a name other than your own. You'll explain this to me too, won't you?*

*There's nothing around here to tell you about because everything
is awful without you. Come back soon. I send you lots of kisses with
my deepest love,*

Jorge

The beginning and end sound a lot like the letters Gabriel sends
to Maricarmen (I've read them all without her knowing, of course),
but I think that overall, it will do. I'm going to copy it out onto my
stationery and give it to Durán to mail.

৯৶

In a year from now, where will I be? What will have happened?
And in ten?

৯৶

I got home today with a split lip and a bloody nose, but I won the
fight. While I was leaving school, I had it out with Oscar (he's
Adelina's brother, that fat girl who badmouths just about everybody, even her own mother, and she's Nena's best friend) because
he said I had been seen making out with Ana Luisa and that I was

making a fool of myself because she gets it on with everybody. I don't believe it and I won't let anyone talk like that. The worst part is that what with the letter and now this, there are already too many mysteries and doubts. I had to say I got into a fight because they were criticizing my father for how he was dealing with the problem of the peasants.

৪৯

Thank god it worked itself out. I'm not sure exactly how, but my father won't have to intervene directly. I'm still waiting for a letter from Ana Luisa. I went to the movies again with Candelaria and Durán. We saw *Symphony in Paris* and *Singing in the Rain.*

৪৯

Nobody comes near me at school. Seems like ever since that thing with Oscar, they're afraid to talk to me or maybe they're just giving me the silent treatment. Even Pablo, who was almost my best friend, tries to make sure the others don't see us together too much.

৪৯

I couldn't stand it any longer so I told Candelaria and Durán all about the mysteries surrounding Ana Luisa. She said that she knew all about it but hadn't mentioned anything because she hadn't wanted to disillusion me; that if she was willing to talk now it was so I would know what to expect. The reason Ana Luisa goes to Xalapa is that her father and the woman he lives with—because her real mother ran away with another man right after Ana Luisa was born—are trying to marry her off to a guy there who she had a relationship with. It was pretty obvious what kind of relationship she was talking about. But they can't make him marry her legally or by force because he's the governor's nephew, and if they turn against her, there won't be any hope at all.

I acted like I was completely indifferent in front of Candelaria and Durán, but inside I feel like I'm going to explode.

৯৯

Dearest Ana Luisa,

Did you get my letter? Why don't you answer it? I must see you and talk to you because some very strange things are going on around here. I beg you to please come back as soon as possible or at least answer me. Even just a note. Do it now, don't put it off until later. I send you many kisses, I miss you more and more every day, and I love you always,

Jorge

৯৯

I never should have confided in Durán. He treats me differently now and takes a lot of liberties he never used to. Anyway . . .

It seems like this thing with Ana Luisa is making me get into fights with everybody. Nobody at school talks to me anymore, but they keep looking at me like I'm some kind of freak. And, what's going on in Xalapa? Why doesn't Ana Luisa write? Could what Candelaria said be true? Couldn't she have made it all up out of jealousy?

৯৯

The telephone rang while I was reading *King Solomon's Mines*. It was Ana Luisa. She just got back from Xalapa today. She very quickly said to me, "Thank you for writing. I've been thinking about you a lot. Meet me after work. Now hand the phone over to Nena so no one will get suspicious." The whole rest of the day and the night are going to be pure misery because I'm dying to see her.

৯৯

Where to begin? Well, Durán didn't want to lend me the car because my father would have gotten mad at him if he had found out, so he suggested that the four of us go out together. He said he would pick Candelaria up, then come to school to get me, and then we'd all stop by The Yardage Paradise for Ana Luisa. Candelaria works near her so she was going to tell her about the arrangements. And that's just what we did.

Ana Luisa was waiting for us at the corner. She didn't seem to care that I hadn't come alone. She greeted Candelaria as if she had known her for years, climbed into the back seat and, without caring if everybody saw, she gave me a kiss.

"Where are we going?" she asked. "I can stay out until eight."

"Anywhere, just for a drive," Durán answered. "How does Antón Lizardo sound?"

"It's too far away," Ana Liusa responded.

"Yeah, but they might see us if we go anywhere else," Candelaria added.

"Oh, what are you talking about? It's not like we're going to be doing, oh, I don't know what!" Ana Luisa said.

"Now, now, my child, you musn't have evil thoughts," Durán immediately responded, with a voice like a Mexican movie actor. "It's just that if they happen to see us and the General finds out, they'll send me to the firing squad for playing the part of his dear little boy's love counselor."

The girls laughed but I didn't. I didn't like Durán's tone of voice. But what could I do? He was doing me a favor and I was totally at his mercy.

Durán went back to Independencia and then drove straight along Díaz Mirón until we got to the Boca del Río and Alvarado Highway. We went right past the La Boticaria Barracks. Durán looked at me through the rearview mirror and warned me, "You'd better duck, kiddo, 'cause if anyone sees you, it's bang-bang."

Now I really had to pretend to laugh, because if I had shown how mad I was I would have made a total fool of myself. But I couldn't stand being treated like a little kid just so he could show off in front of the girls.

I was sitting about a foot away from Ana Luisa. I looked at her but didn't dare move any closer or open my mouth. After writing her those letters, I didn't know what to say or how to talk to her in front of other people. Durán, on the other hand, was driving like a madman, and Candelaria was practically sitting on his lap, and every once in a while he looked back at us through the rearview mirror.

Ana Luisa seemed to be very amused by the whole situation. She smiled, but she didn't say anything either. Then finally she said, loud enough for the others to hear, "Come closer. I don't bite."

I didn't like that little comment, but I took advantage of the opportunity to move closer to her, put my arm around her, hold her hand, and kiss her on the mouth. I tried to do it silently, but there was a smack anyway. Durán turned around and said, "That's the way, my children, excellent. Carry on."

He sounded like such a moron, I felt like saying, "What's it your business anyway, you son-of-a-bitch?" But I controlled myself because if I'd gotten into a fight with him it would have ruined everything, and the most important thing was that Ana Luisa and I were going to be, at least almost, alone together.

It must have been about six-thirty when we got to the beach. We went way past where the fishermen keep their nets and boats. We got out of the car, and the two girls went ahead to look at something in the sand, and Durán turned to me and said under his breath, "If you don't get it on with her now, you really are a stupid ass. That girl's already been around so much she's almost worn out . . ."

I couldn't control myself any longer. That was the last straw and he'd never spoken to me like that before so I said, "I'd shut my mouth if I were you. What the fuck business is it of yours anyway?"

He didn't say a word. He and Candelaria went back to the car. Ana Luisa and I walked away along the edge of the water holding hands. Then we sat down on a log at the foot of the sand dunes.

"I want to ask you a few questions," I said.

"I don't feel like talking. And anyway, haven't you been dying to be alone with me? Well, here I am, now's your chance, let's not waste any time."

"Okay, but I'd like to know . . . ."

"Oh boy, you've probably been hearing all kinds of stupid gossip. Just don't pay any attention to it. What? Don't you love me? Don't you trust me?"

"I adore you," and I hugged her and kissed her on the mouth. My tongue touched hers, I pulled her very close to me and began caressing her.

"I love you, I love you, you're fantastic," she said in a tone of voice I had never heard her use before.

And before I knew it, it was already dark and we were rolling around in the sand. I put my hand under her blouse, I touched her legs, and I was about to take off her skirt (boy, if anyone sees this notebook, I'm in deep trouble, but I have to write down everything that happened today) when suddenly a bright light shone right into our eyes.

I thought: It's one of Durán's jokes. But it wasn't. The car was parked a long way away and the lights were off. It was a school bus on its way to the beach. I have no idea what they were going to do there at that time of day. Maybe they were going to look for sea urchins for an experiment or something. Who knows!

We quickly got up and walked along the edge of the water holding hands as if nothing had happened. The bus parked near us and a whole bunch of little girls in gray uniforms and two nuns got off. They gave us such nasty, dirty looks that we had to go back to the car and try to brush off the sand that was all over us, even in our ears. Candelaria was brushing her hair, and Durán was hitching up his pants.

"Those stupid bitches came and spoiled the party," he said.

"Let's go somewhere else," I suggested.

"No, it's too late. We'd better get back," Ana Luisa said.

"Yeah, we really should. Just think what would happen if your Dad caught us," Durán added.

"What about it?"

"He'll get really pissed off, raise a big stink, and the four of us would never be able to go out together again."

Durán's attitude had changed. It was a good thing I had had the guts to stop him when I did. The return trip was kind of sad. Nobody spoke. But I had my arms around Ana Luisa, and I touched her everywhere without caring if they saw us. We dropped her off around the corner from her house. She left without saying when we would see each other again.

Right after Candelaria got out, Durán took me to a bathroom in a restaurant. I washed my face and brushed my hair. I put white powder on my lips—they were so swollen!—and lotion in my hair. I didn't know Durán always carried those things around with him in the glove compartment.

Of course there was a big row when we got back. Durán came through though. He said that he had been giving me a driving lesson and we had had a flat tire. I've written a lot and I'm exhausted. I can't go on anymore.

ૐ

Unlike yesterday, today was horrible. I was *out of it* in class. Then my mother said, "I know you're going out with *that girl*. I'm just warning you, she's bad news." I'd like to know how she found out.

ૐ

Ana Luisa and I met at seven-thirty. She was very affectionate to me and begged me to promise her that we wouldn't go out with Durán and Candelaria anymore. The problem is that I can't get the car any other way. I didn't have the guts to question her about what Candelaria had told me. It would be awful if Ana Luisa thought I didn't trust her. She told me that my sisters had been very rude to her. That shows that at home everyone knows everything . . . But I wouldn't leave Ana Luisa for anything in the world.

ॐ

I was a total idiot in class again today. I'm even getting worse in the subjects I used to be good at. It's going to be a disaster when my father sees my grades. I can't study or read or concentrate, and I'm always thinking about Ana Luisa and stuff like that.

ॐ

Why is it that Ana Luisa always asks me questions and never wants to tell me anything about herself or her family? It seems like she's ashamed of her father, who has one of those cars with loudspeakers and drives all over the state selling corn-removal ointment, hair dye, and medicine for malaria and worms. There's nothing wrong with that kind of work. I'm the one who should be ashamed of my father, who has made his living killing people. But she doesn't like him very much because he's never home and, since she's an only child, he put her to work when she was very young. Ana Luisa would like to go back to school. She's very intelligent, it's just that she only went to the fourth grade, so she only reads comic books. She knows *Cancionero Picot* by heart, she listens to radio soap operas, and she adores Pedro Infante and Libertad Lamarque movies. I make fun of her sometimes because of her taste, but I think that's wrong because it's not her fault if she was never taught anything different. At least I defended her the other day when Adelina

laughed at her because they went to see *Ambition That Kills* and
Ana Luisa didn't understand it because she didn't have time to read
the subtitles in Spanish. (Ana Luisa told me her version of *Quo
Vadis?*, and it's enough to make you want to cry.) Ana Luisa's lack
of education is a problem, but it can be dealt with, and anyway she
has many other qualities that make up for it. What right do I have
to criticize her? I love her and that's all that matters.

౿౷

A horrible day. Ana Luisa went to Xalapa again. There was a storm,
and the streets and the garden of the house were flooded. I got into
a fight with Nena because she said, "Hey, why don't you get yourself a decent girlfriend and stop making a spectacle of yourself
with that chick who makes it with everybody." Fortunately nobody
else was around, but I'm sure Nena is going to tell my mother that
I swore at her, and she and Adelina will make fun of me because
I said I was proud of Ana Luisa and that I loved her a lot.

౿౷

I was so sad on Sunday when I woke up, I didn't even have the
strength to get out of bed. I pretended I had a headache and a sore
throat so I could spend hours and hours thinking about what Ana
Luisa was doing and when she would return from Xalapa. The
worst part was when my mother rubbed my chest with anti-inflam-
matory cream and I almost vomited.

౿౷

Complete humiliation. The principal sent for me. He said my grades
keep plummeting and that my behavior in and out of school is scan-
dalous. If I don't shape up, he will speak to my father and recom-
mend that I be sent off to military school. Then that damn sissy
creep proceeded to give me a full-length sermon to the effect that

I was too young to be running around with women because they will only be my ruin and turn me into a "human rag." Does that son-of-a-bitch really think I haven't seen his eyes pop out of his head when he looks at girls' legs? I kept my cool, glued my eyes on the floor, and repeated again and again, being the kiss-ass that I am, "Yes sir, Mr. Principal, I promise it will never happen again." And to top it off, he gave me a few slaps on the back with the greasy palm of his hand and said, "You're made out of the right stuff, son. We all make mistakes. I'm sure you will soon be back on the right track. Go on now, go back to class." So, I guess the whole world knows about Ana Luisa and me and everybody, absolutely everybody, is against us. What the hell do they care?! Oh, if I could I would burn down the whole damn school and kill all those jerks who only teach us bullshit.

୬ଈ

Everything's still the same. I miss Ana Luisa. What's she going to do? When will she return? Why doesn't she write?

୬ଈ

Things are going from bad to worse. We went to eat at Boca del Río: the whole family and a really beautiful friend of Nena and Maricarmen named Yolanda, and they kept making insinuations, saying that Gilberto (Yolanda's brother, a real jerk who's buddy-buddy with Pablo) is always going out with housemaids instead of getting interested in the girls at his school. "I guess those servant girls must have their own special charms," Maricarmen said, looking me straight in the eye. "Because I can assure you that Gilberto isn't the only one we know who runs after that kind of girl."

I wanted to throw my hot soup in her face. Luckily, my mother changed the subject. Maricarmen forgets that her dear Gabriel is a poor slob even though he does have a lot of money, and the only boyfriend Nena's been able to get is a lowly captain. What they'd really like to do is get me hooked up with Adelina. What a nightmare! I'd rather die than put up with that elephant!

જ⊷

My father hasn't been home for three days. My mother cries all day. I asked Maricarmen what's going on. She said, "Don't butt into things that are none of your business."

જ⊷

My father returned. He said he went to Xalapa to work some things out with the governor. Durán went with him and knows the whole truth, but he won't tell me anything. Maybe he saw Ana Luisa? No, that's impossible. *I* don't even have her address.

જ⊷

I've been saved by a miracle. When the mailman came, I was home alone. When I picked up the mail I noticed an envelope without a return address. I opened it even though it was addressed to my father and could have turned out to be just a regular letter. But my intuition didn't fail me: it was an anonymous letter, composed with letters cut out of *El Dictamen,* and sloppily glued onto the paper. It said:

ONE, TWO, THREE. TESTING, TESTING. THE UPSTANDING CITIZENS OF VERACRUZ ARE SCANDALIZED BY YOU AND YOUR SON'S BEHAVIOR. IF THIS IS WHAT THE BOY IS DOING NOW, WHAT WILL HE DO WHEN HE GROWS UP? SEND HIM OFF TO A REFORM SCHOOL AS SOON AS POSSIBLE. DON'T LET HIM FOLLOW IN YOUR FOOTSTEPS. HERE WE ARE ALL DECENT HARD-WORKING PEOPLE. WHY DO THEY ALWAYS SEND US PEOPLE LIKE YOU FROM MEXICO CITY?

WE REFUSE TO ACCEPT CORRUPT FAMILIES LIKE YOURS. LIKE
FATHER, LIKE SON. WE ARE WATCHING. WE WILL KEEP YOU IN-
FORMED. THE WALLS ARE LISTENING. EVERYTHING IS KNOWN.
NO CRIME GOES UNPUNISHED. HE WHO SWIMS IN SIN SHALL SINK
IN SIN. DO YOU UNDERSTAND? SHAPE UP OR SHIP OUT.

I'm going to burn it right now and bury the ashes in the garden. I'd
never before seen a real anonymous letter. I thought they only
existed in Mexican movies. I can't imagine who could have sent it.
It couldn't have been any of my classmates or any of my sisters'
friends. (I've heard that Adelina sends anonymous letters, but I
don't think she would dare send one to my father.) None of them
would have the patience to cut out all those letters and then spend
hours sticking them onto paper. Anyway, there are some words in
it that nobody I know would use. It sounds like the way the principal talks, and he listens to radio soap operas; but how can he talk
in the name of the upstanding citizens of Veracruz when he isn't
even from here. He wouldn't want to get mixed up like that with
my father anyway. He knows my father would be perfectly capable
of putting a bullet through his brains. And even though I do hate
him, I don't think he would stoop so low as to send an anonymous
letter.

৯০

I keep going over it in my head and I still can't believe it. Maybe
I'm mistaken and have interpreted everything in the wrong way.
Who knows? What happened is that I went to see if Candelaria had
received a letter from Ana Luisa for me. I'd never seen her without
Durán, and since the pharmacy was full of people she called me
over to one end of the counter, gave me all kinds of insinuating
looks, and said, "You take things too seriously. You should have

fun and enjoy yourself and stop being so old-fashioned. When do you want to sit down and talk things over? I have some good advice to give you."

"Whenever you want. Let's find out when it's good for Durán."

"No, don't say anything to him. Don't even tell him we've talked. It's better if we just meet alone, the two of us. What do you think?"

"Well, you know, I mean, I don't know . . . you're his girlfriend, aren't you?"

"Yes, but we're not glued to each other. What's wrong with you and me seeing each other? I really like you, you know that? Durán's an okay guy but he's kind of a slob. Not like you. You're so refined and good-looking, not a roughneck like him."

"Well, listen, to tell you the truth, I don't know what to think. This all makes me very sad."

"Sad. Why sad? Just remember, my dear, that after all is said and done, Durán works for you, he is *your* servant, ser-vant. I know, you think he's your friend, but you wouldn't believe all the things he says about you and your family. He says that you're a spoiled brat and a dummy on top of it; that your father is a tyrant and a thief who makes money off everything, including the troops' grub, and that he spends it all on women; and that your sisters are loose . . .

Candelaria would have kept on bad-mouthing Durán but the owner called to her and told her not to talk to people during work. We said good-bye.

"Call me here or come by my house. You know where to find me. I don't have a telephone."

What should I do? Should I call her or not? NO. Why get myself messed up in more problems? And anyway, I could never betray Ana Luisa and Durán like that.

ॐ

My dear Ana Luisa,
How are you? Why don't you write? I miss you very much. I
need you. Come back soon. I have to see you. I send you many
kisses and all my love.

Jorge

&

I had just finished writing that out on a post card (and putting it in
an envelope) when Durán arrived, very mysteriously, and handed
me a letter Candelaria had given him in the morning. It seemed to
me like they'd steamed it open and then closed it again with glue
or paste. I shouldn't be so distrustful. I'll copy it here word for
word:

Dear Jorge, I'm sory I havent writen very much but Im taking
care of my father, he took sick all of a sudden but thank god its
nothing serius, hell be ok real soon, then Ill came back.
Jorge Im very sad without you, I think youll forget about me and
look at other girls who wont cause you so many problems like me.
But you beter not because I love you very much you cant imagine
how much, Im dying to see you hopfuly real soon. Good by Jorge,
I send many kisses and my love thats always for you and love
me too

Ana Luisa

Well, I don't know what to think. And anyway, how could Ana
Luisa know that she's caused me so many problems?

This was bound to happen sooner or later: Somebody told my father
the whole story. Who could it have been? Nena swears it wasn't
her, and so does Maricarmen. I believe her because she is, at least,
honest and straightforward. So, could it have been someone from
school? I don't think so.

This was much worse than with the principal. He said that as long as he is supporting me, my duty is to study and obey, that afterward when I'm working and earning my own money I can have thousands of women; but that this is the worst thing to do and he's telling me from his own personal experience (wow!).

My father might be a general or whatever else, but he sure doesn't understand what's going on. He told me that from now on and until he gives further orders, I can't go anywhere without being accompanied and chaperoned by Durán(!).

᠃❧

A little while ago I snuck out of the house from the roof to go spy on Ana Luisa's house just like I do every night, and I saw her get out of a brand new Packard (I know that car) with the woman she lives with. They didn't see me because I hid around the corner. I'm dying of curiosity to find out who that middle-aged guy is who dropped them off. He helped them with their bags and kissed Ana Luisa on the cheek when he said good-bye. But he didn't go into the house.

I feel so desperate not being able to talk to her! I hope she sends me a message tomorrow through Candelaria. I would love to go pick her up or at least call her at work and talk to her, but she forbade me to because she said they yell at her and then take it out of her paycheck.

Now here's another very strange thing: If the owner of the store is so strict, how is it that he lets her miss so much work? Why doesn't he just fire her and hire somebody else? I've never known anyone as mysterious as Ana Luisa.

᠃❧

This is what I least expected. Ana Luisa left a little pink envelope with Candelaria for Durán to give to me:

Dear Jorge, I got your card, thanks. I hope that what Im going to tell you doesnt bother you because it makes me real sad but theres no other way and I think its the best for both of us.

It looks like we arent going to keep seeing each other Jorge like we have been until now I know youll understand and wont ask for explanashons cause I couldn't give you any. Jorge Ive always been sinceer with you Ive really loved you, youll never really know how much. Itll be very hard to forget you and I just hope your not going to suffer like Im suffering and that you can forget me. Im sending you a last kiss with all my love.

Ana Luisa

I went numb all over. Then I locked myself in my room and started crying like a two-year-old. Now I'm trying to calm down and am making a great effort to write in this book. I can't believe it, I can't stand the idea that I'll never see Ana Luisa again. It's horrible, it's terrible, and I don't know what to think. I just don't know, I don't understand anything.

ॐ

I spent a hellish night. Durán took me to school in the jeep and we didn't speak, but I'm absolutely positive he already knows and maybe even saw the letter because it was in an unsealed envelope. Candelaria didn't have the delicacy to close it.

Aftr school, I hung out around where Ana Luisa works—or used to work. I saw her friends, but not her. I went to talk to them, but they said she hasn't been at the store, and they don't think she'll ever come back. I felt like going to her house, but on what pretext? I don't care if I make a fool of myself, I just want to see her one last time.

ॐ

My mother came into my room without knocking and found me crying (at my age). She asked me what was going on, and I gave her an edited version of the story. Instead of scolding me, she told me not to worry, that she had known about it all along and hadn't put a stop to it because she had wanted it to be a learning experience for me; that things like that have happened or will happen to everybody, and I shouldn't make too big a deal out of it. Soon I would find a girl from a family like ours who could be my real girlfriend and who doesn't have as bad a reputation as Ana Luisa.

This time I didn't even put up a fight like I used to. I didn't even try to defend her. Poor Ana Luisa! Everybody wants to hurt her. Now I realize that I never really knew anything about her. I don't think I could fall in love with anybody else . . . And what if everything changes and Ana Luisa comes and tells me she thought it over, reconsidered, and regrets what she has done? No, that's foolishness, it isn't going to happen and it doesn't do me any good to have those kinds of illusions.

ॐ

Days, weeks without writing anything in this book. Why should I? There's no point to it. If somebody sees it, they'll just make fun of me.

ॐ

I had a very sad dream that was absolutely vivid. We were in Mexico City. Ana Luisa had agreed to meet me at La Bella Italia so I could see her one last time, because she was going away and was never going to come back. We were supposed to meet at twelve. I took a streetcar and it stopped because there wasn't enough light; then a truck came by and crashed into it. I started running along a tree-lined street—Amsterdam? Alvaro Obregón? Mazatlán?—until my legs started hurting and I had to sit down on a bench. At that moment, Nena appeared arm-in-arm with Durán. "We're on our way to church to get married," she said. "And you, where are you going in such a hurry? Don't tell me you're going to see Ana Luisa." I said no, that I was going to a soccer game, and they kept chatting with me, and I was desperate to get away. Finally I started running again, and I came across a funeral procession. On the corner there was a woman in mourning. It was my mother and she began to scold me. "They're about to bury your father and instead of mourning him at the cemetery, you're running off to meet that slut." I said I was sorry and kept running. When I got to La Bella Italia it was exactly twelve o'clock, but Ana Luisa wasn't there. Candelaria appeared as a waitress with an apron. She told me that Ana Luisa had waited for me for a long time, but that she had to go away forever and hadn't said where she was going . . .

ॐ

Two months without seeing her, six weeks since I received her last letter. Instead of forgetting her, I feel like I love her more than ever. And I don't care if that sounds corny.

ॐ

I wrote her a poem, but it was so bad I tore it up. What is she doing? Where is she and who is she with? I go by her house every night. It's always locked up. Did she go back to Xalapa? Did she go to Mexico City?

ॐ

The saddest part of all is that I'm beginning to resign myself to the situation. I guess that sooner or later this thing with Ana Luisa had to come to an end, since at my age I wasn't going to marry her or anything like that. Anyway, since we stopped seeing each other, everything seems so peaceful. People at school talk to me, they treat me better at home, I can study, I'm reading a lot, and as far as I know, no more anonymous letters have come to the house. But I wouldn't care if everything went back to the way it was, or even worse, as long as I could be near Ana Luisa.

&

I'm worried about Ana Luisa. It hurts me that I can't do anything for her. I guess things aren't going so well for her and her life is going to be awful and it's not even her fault. But then again, when you really think about it and look carefully at the people you know or have heard about, everybody's life is always pretty awful.

&

The things we had left behind in Mexico City have arrived and they included a trunk where my mother keeps the photographs. Instead of studying or reading, I spent hours looking through them. It's difficult for me to accept the fact that I am the same person as that child who appears in those photos from so many years ago. One day, I am going to be as old as my parents and then all of this I've been through, this whole story with Ana Luisa, will seem unbelievable and even sadder than it does now. I don't understand why life is the way it is. But then again, I can't imagine how it could be any different.

&

It's twelve-thirty. I didn't go to school. Today is my father's birthday. The governor, the mayor, and I don't know who else, are coming over. Instead of Eusebio preparing the food like he does every day, a special cook has been hired. I'm not going to eat a single bite of anything. I don't think I'm ever going to eat again. I'm so dumb that at my age I still hadn't realized the connection between death and suffering and the food we eat. I watched the cook killing the animals, and I was horrified. The most disgusting thing was the way the turtles die or maybe it's the poor lobsters that flop around desperately in the pot of boiling water. We should eat only bread, vegetables, and fruit. But do you really think they don't feel anything when you bite into them and chew them up?

ঽ�

Yolanda came by to say good-bye to my sisters because she's going to study in Switzerland. And Gilberto is being sent off to a military academy in Illinois. His father became a millionaire during this government that's now on its way out. So have a lot of other people we know. If most people in Mexico are so poor, where do they get it all? How do some of them manage to steal so much?

Yolanda told us that a few days ago Adelina tried to commit suicide. She stuck her head in the oven and turned on the gas. She changed her mind when she started feeling sick and ran outside, but she vomited all over the living room before she fainted.

Adelina had left a note behind: She blamed her suicide on her mother and her brother and the captain gave Oscar a beating. Poor captain! He loves Adelina so much and he doesn't even realize that his daughter is a monster.

Nena, Maricarmen, and I laughed our heads off while Yolanda was telling the story and acting out Adelina's tragedy. Then I felt guilty: It's wrong to derive pleasure from another's misfortune, no matter how much I hate Oscar and Adelina and even though I am almost positive she was the one who sent the anonymous letter and carefully planned it out so that we would blame it on the principal.

ঽ�

I don't understand myself. The other day, I felt great compassion while I watched the cook killing the animals, and today I had great fun stepping on crabs at the beach. Not the big ones that live in the rocks; the little gray sand crabs. They would run around madly looking for their holes and I would crush them furiously and just for the fun of it. Then I thought that in some ways we are all like crabs and when we least expect it, someone or something comes along and crushes us.

ॐ

I haven't gone out with Candelaria and Durán, and I didn't even know if they were still seeing each other. Durán and I don't talk much. I feel like somehow I have betrayed someone who (except for the day at Antón Lizardo) has been good to me. I think he knows something about that conversation in the pharmacy because he hasn't made any effort to talk to me or go swimming with me or take me out driving.

Anyway, I'm saying all this because today I ran into Candelaria on the streetcar, and I decided to invite her for a soda at the Yucatán so I could talk to her about Ana Luisa. We had just sat down when Candelaria asked me about her.

"You mean you really don't know? I can't believe it. Well, she broke up with me, she told me to get lost."

"You're kidding! I didn't know anything about it."

"But, how is that possible? She left the letter with you."

"I didn't read it, of course, I'm very discreet . . . What an idiot, what a fool, when is she going to find someone else like you?"

"What are you talking about? I'm a nobody."

"You are you, and I already told you what I think about you."

Silence. I blush. I take a sip of my tamarind drink. Candelaria watches me; she enjoys making things tough for me.

"I can tell you one thing. Your mistake was treating her like a decent girl and not like what she really is."

"Listen, she's never done anything to you. You have no reason to talk that way about her."

"Well, will you look at him. After she cheats on you and throws you away like an old rag, you still stick up for her. Oh, my dear boy, you are either very good or very stupid. If only everyone were like you. That's why I like you, that's why . . . But you don't want to have anything to do with me . . ."

"It's just that . . . I don't know, I mean . . . No, let's wait until after my exams. I have to study a lot. As soon as that's all over, we'll talk."

"And why not right now?"

"My parents are waiting for me to eat at La Parroquia. Anyway, you have to get back to the pharmacy."

"Don't worry about me, I can take care of myself."

"It's better if we see each other next week, don't you think? But please, don't say anything to Durán."

"Relax, he won't hear a word. Anyway, I'm sick and tired of Durán. I don't know how to get rid of him. He's a big pain and he thinks he's the eighth wonder of the world. He's just got a big mouth, that's all."

Before anything else could happen, I paid the bill, said good-bye, repeated that my parents were waiting for me, and promised her that I would go visit her at her house. Instead of feeling happy, the conversation made me sad. Everything is so unfair: the girl I love rejects me, and I reject the girl who loves me. Maybe I'm just deceiving myself by believing it's this way. Could what Candelaria says be true? Maybe she just wants to use me to get back at Durán?

ॐ

I haven't written anything here for a long time, but now I'm going to make up for all the days I left blank. Something terrible just happened to me. It will be better if I try to tell it more or less in order. Since there's no school tomorrow and my grades have gotten a lot better, I asked for permission to go to the wrestling match.

They said okay, but only if I went with Durán and, believe it or not, that is what ended up saving me.

We managed to buy scalped fifth-row tickets. The preliminaries were boring: all unknown fighters. But the star attraction was a fight between Bill Montenegro—my idol—and El Verdugo Rojo—the villain I hate most in the world.

Even though the referee was against him from the start, Bill had the advantage all through the first round and won it by letting go a few perfect flying kicks and then a double nelson. In the second round, El Verdugo used all of his dirty tricks and gave Montenegro a good kicking. By the third and last round, everybody in the audience was against the dimwit except Durán, who took his side—I think—just to spite me.

Montenegro fell outside the ring and banged his head. El Verdugo picked him up by his hair, held him in a headlock, and bashed him against the ring posts until he split his head wide open. Then, covered in blood, Bill turned on him and, with a combination of scissor kicks and butts, he got back at his enemy by throwing him outside the ring. They were hitting each other in the aisle right next to me. The referee forced them back into the ring because the audience was starting to interfere and take sides with Montenegro.

But Bill's downfall began with his return to the ring. His masked opponent threw him against the post again and opened up his wound. I got furious seeing him bleeding so much, and since the referee didn't pay any attention to all the protests, I threw the corn-on-the-cob I was eating and it hit El Verdugo Rojo on the head.

Everybody who realized what I'd done applauded me. But then the villain grabbed the corn and started scratching at Bill's eyes with such fury it was a miracle he didn't scratch them out. The same people who had just been applauding, started swearing at me, and then things got worse when El Verdugo knocked Bill out completely with a break.

The audience threw pillows and paper cups at El Verdugo. They took Montenegro away, half-dead, to the infirmary. Then some guys came over and wanted to beat me up. They were shouting that it was all my fault that Bill lost. There were about twenty of them, and it seemed like they were going to lynch me. I was terrified. They had already gone so far as to break up some chairs when Durán pulled out his pistol and shouted, "If you want him, you're going to have to deal with me first, you sons-of-bitches."

I don't know what would have happened if the police hadn't arrived and pushed their way through the crowd. Durán showed them his ID and explained the situation, told them who I was, in other words, who my father was, and we were escorted out by the policemen and followed by angry glares.

As we got into the jeep, Durán gave them fifty pesos and then said to me, "You can pay me back later. The most important thing is that the boss doesn't find out about this." And then he told me that what I had done was an act of supreme idiocy, that you always have to think of yourself first and never take sides. I didn't answer because at that moment all at once I was beginning to feel afraid. What a night!

&

I'm writing in this book for the last time. Frankly, I don't see any point in only writing about disasters. But I'll keep it so I can read it many years from now. Hopefully, someday I'll be able to laugh at it all. Everything that happened today seems so unbelievable and hurt me so much that I feel kind of like I've been anesthetized and like I'm seeing everything through a pane of glass.

All on my own, I went out looking for the catastrophe, as usual. There weren't any classes today and I don't know why or how, but I got it into my head to go to Mocambo. Alone, of course, since I don't have any friends at school, and since today was Durán's day off and my father was staying home in bed, he lent him the jeep. I couldn't get the big car because my mother and Nena and Maricarmen went to Tlacotalpan to a festival for poor children.

I got on the bus in Villa del Mar and sat down on the sunny side. It was terribly hot and when I got off, I went to get a drink at a stand on the beach. I sat down, ordered a Coca-Cola with lemon sherbet and started to read *The Twenty-fifth Hour* (whenever I go anywhere alone, I always bring a book or a magazine).

My book was so interesting that at first I didn't even notice how smashed the two guys were who were sitting at the table in front of me. They had already drunk about one hundred Cuba libres, and they were slurring their words and hugging each other. When I finally looked up, I was shocked: It was Bill Montenegro and El Verdugo Rojo (without his mask, but I recognized his muscles). So, it truns out that wrestling is just a big put-on, and the same people who are mortal enemies in the ring are best buddies in their private lives!

They didn't even bother to look around to see the fool who almost got killed because of them. I felt like telling off Montenegro, but he was on the verge of passing out and they would have killed me if I had started to tell them off.

I left the stand and decided that I would never again go to another one of those farces or buy another sports magazine in my whole life. But the best was yet to come. I went into the pine grove to drop off my clothes and my book before going into the water. Just as I was taking off my pants, Ana Luisa and Durán, in bathing suits and holding hands, walked past me.

They kept right on going without seeing me. Near the shore, Ana Luisa lay down on the sand and Durán, right out there in the open in front of everybody, started to rub tanning oil on her legs and back and on the way gave her kisses on her neck and mouth.

I was shaking, but I couldn't move. It seemed like the end of a bad movie or a nightmare. Because it's impossible for so many things to happen on this earth, at least not all at once. It was un-believable, but true. There, just a few steps away from me, were Ana Luisa and Durán making out in public, and Bill Montenegro and El Verdugo Rojo were back there at the drink stand.

I had to leave. If I didn't, I would have only added ridicule to fear and disillusionment. Just walk away: What else could I do? Fight with Durán, knowing he'd finish me off by the count of three? I couldn't tell Ana Luisa off: She had told me very clearly that she didn't want anything more to do with me, and once that was said, she was free. How could I feel betrayed by her, by Durán, by Mon-tenegro? Ana Luisa didn't ask me to fall in love with her, and Montenegro didn't ask me to "defend" him from El Verdugo Rojo. It isn't anybody's fault that I didn't know that everything is just a show, a big farce.

I said all these things to myself to give me courage. Because I have never felt so bad in all my life, so humiliated, stupid, like such a coward. Then I thought of a quick revenge. With my last ten pesos, I paid for a taxi and went to Candelaria's house.

I knocked on the door because there was no bell. No one an-swered. I was about to leave when suddenly a shutter opened and a man's head appeared in the window. He had a mustache and was all sweaty, and his hair was a mess. I guess it was her stepfather, and he shouted at me in the rudest possible voice, "What do you want, kid?"

Like an idiot, I said, "Excuse me . . . Is Candelaria home?"

"No, she's not. What do you want her for?"

"No, nothing. Excuse, me . . . I mean . . . yes . . . look, sir . . . I have a message for her from Durán . . . her boyfriend. Well, it doesn't matter, I'll talk to her tomorrow at the pharmacy."

The old grouch slammed the shutter angrily, and the whole win-dowframe shook. That supposed revenge of mine sure was a stupid move. I thought that if I stayed outside today, I would be crushed by a meteor or a tidal wave would wash me away or something like that. I walked home feeling like crying, but I controlled myself, and I felt like telling everything and everybody to go to hell and I wanted to write it all down and save it to see if one day in the future all of this that is so tragic now will seem like a comedy . . . But who knows. If, according to my mother, what I'm living now "is the happiest period of my life," what must the others be like, god-damn it.

YOU WOULDN'T UNDERSTAND

S	he took my hand as we crossed the street, and I felt the dampness of her palm.

"I want to play in the park for a while."

"No. It's too late. We have to get home; your mother is waiting for us. Look, there's nobody else around. All the little children are home in bed."

The streetlight changed. The cars moved forward. We ran across the street. The smell of exhaust dissolved into the freshness of grass and foliage. The last remnants of rain evaporated or were absorbed by the sprouts, leaves, roots, nervations.

"Are there going to be any mushrooms?"

"Yes, I guess so."

"When?"

"Well, I guess by tomorrow there should be some."

"Will you bring me here to see them?"

"Yes, but you'll have to go to bed right away so you can get up early."

I walked too quickly, and the child had to hurry to keep up with me. She stopped, lifted her eyes, looked at me to gain courage, and asked, slightly embarrassed, "Daddy, do dwarfs really exist?"

43

"Well, they do in stories."

"And witches?"

"Yes, but also just in stories."

"That's not true."

"Why?"

"I've seen witches on TV, and they scare me a lot."

"They shouldn't. Everything you see on television is also stories—with witches—made up to entertain children, not scare them."

"Oh, so everything they show on TV is just stories?"

"No, not everything. I mean . . . how can I explain it to you? You wouldn't understand."

Night fell. A livid firmament fluted with grayish clouds. In the garbage cans, Sunday's refuse began to decay: newspapers, beer cans, sandwich wrappers. Beyond the distant drone of traffic, raindrops could be heard falling from the leaves and tree trunks onto the grass. The path wound through a clearing between two groves of trees. At that moment, the shouts reached my ears: ten or twelve boys had surrounded another. With his back against the tree, he looked at them with fear but did not scream for help or mercy.

My daughter grabbed my hand again.

"What are they doing?"

"I don't know. Fighting. Let's go. Come on, hurry up."

The fragile pressure of her fingers was like a reproach. She had figured it out: I was accountable to her. At the same time, my daughter represented an alibi, a defense against fear and excessive guilt.

We stood absolutely still. I managed to see the face—the dark skin reddened by white hands—of the boy who was being festively beaten by the others. I shouted at them to stop. Only one of them turned around to look at me, and he made a threatening, scornful gesture. The girl watched all of this without blinking. The boy fell, and they kicked him on the ground. Someone picked him up, and the others kept slugging him. I did not dare move. I wanted to believe that if I did not intervene, it was to protect my daughter, because I knew there was nothing I could do against all twelve of them.

"Daddy, tell them to stop. Scold them."

"Don't move. Wait here for me."

Before I finished speaking, they were already running quickly away, dispersing in all directions. I felt obscenely liberated. I cherished the cowardly hope that my daughter would think they had run away from me. We approached. The boy rose with difficulty. He was bleeding from his nose and mouth.

"Let me help you. I'll take you . . ."

He looked at me without answering. He wiped the blood off with the cuffs of his checkered shirt. I offered him a handkerchief. Not even a no: disgust in his eyes. Something—an undefinable horror—in the girl's expression. Both of their faces were an aura of deceit, a pain of betrayal.

He turned his back on us. He walked away dragging his feet. For a moment I thought he would collapse. He continued until he disappeared among the trees. Silence.

"Let's go. Let's get out of here."

"Why did they do that to him if he wasn't doing anything to them?"

"I guess because they were fighting."

"But there were lots of them."

"I know. I know."

"They're bad because they hit him, right?"

"Of course. That's the wrong thing to do."

The park seemed to go on forever. We would never reach the bus. We would never return home. She would never stop asking me questions nor I giving her the same answers they undoubtedly gave me at her age.

"So, that means he's good?"

"Who?"

"The boy the others made bleed?"

"Yes, I mean, I don't know."

"Or is he bad too?"

"No, no. The others are the bad ones because of what they did."

Finally we found a policeman. I described to him what I had just witnessed.

"There's nothing to be done. It happens every night. You did the right thing by not interfering. They are always armed and can be dangerous. They claim the park is only for whites and that any dirty nigger who steps foot in here will suffer the consequences."

"But they don't have the right, they can't do that."

"What are you talking about? That's what the people in the neighborhood say. But when it comes down to it, they won't let blacks come to their houses or sit in their bars."

He gave the child an affectionate pat and continued on his way. I understood that clichés like "the world's indifference" were not totally meaningless. Three human beings—the victim, my daughter, myself—had just been dramatically affected by something about which nobody else seemed to care.

I was cold, tired, and felt like closing my eyes. We reached the edge of the park. Three black boys crossed the street with us. No one had ever looked at me like that. I saw their switchblades and thought they were going to attack us. But they kept going and disappeared into the grove.

"Daddy, what are they going to do?"

"Not let happen to them what happened to the other one."

"But why do they always have to fight?"

"I can't explain it to you, it's too difficult, you wouldn't understand."

I knelt down to button up her coat. I hugged her gently, with tenderness and fear. The dampness of the trees encircled us. The park was advancing upon the city and again—or overtly—everything would be jungle.

THE SUNKEN PARK

> Childhood is miserable because every evil is still ahead.
> —Denis Donaghue

Every afternoon after school he looked at the sunken park, the long, green expanse growing unevenly alongside the street. But today he descended the stairway and crossed the lonely clearing until he reached the pool of green, stagnant water.

Standing by the edge of the reservoir covered with lime and inhabited by fish and frogs, he lifted his eyes and looked at the sky that cast shadows over the grove as the clouds thickened.

He felt lonely. He retraced his steps and climbed the slope. He looked back at the park, then continued along his way as if he were escaping.

"Don't eat it if you don't like it. But I'm not going to let you take things out of the refrigerator on your own anymore."

His Aunt Florence cleared away the plate. Arthur took a few sips of the cold milk. He fingered the crumbs that remained on the table.

He was about to turn nine years old, and his world had been reduced to Florence, the one-story house, the cat who would not let itself be petted by him and had killed its own kittens, the Juan A. Mateos School, and Rafael Molina, his classmate who accompanied him to the movies and on frog-catching expeditions in the park.

(Months previously, Arthur had brought home a toad wrapped in a damp cloth. Florence had slapped his wrists and flushed the

51

toad down the toilet. Not long afterward, the cat devoured the white
mouse Arthur had bought on his way home from school.)

He went back into the living room. He picked up his arithmetic
notebook and began solving fraction problems. When he had finished, he left his pencil next to the portrait of the man who came
every Saturday to visit him, kissed him, and gave him a little bit of
money: the man Arthur could never call "Daddy" despite his gentle
insistence that he do so.

One night, through the closed door, he overheard a conversation
he would have preferred not to. He was about to fall asleep when
Florence shuffled the cards in the living room for one of the women
who paid her to tell the future.

"She hasn't seen him for seven years. Of course, we would never
allow it. Ricardo has a family now, and the past is over and done
with. The child is no bother at all. He has been with me ever since
and, as you can see, I'm taking care of him just as I did my own
brother. The worst part is, though, Luisita, that the money Ricardo
gives me isn't nearly enough. And I can't ask him for any more. He
has a lot of expenses with his wife and daughters. But I have to try
to make ends meet however possible . . . shuffle seven times, now
cut the cards, now touch them here . . ."

"Did you say your prayers?" Florence asked him as she came into
the room carrying the cat that rubbed up against her body.

"No, not yet."

"Kneel and pray. Come on, let's do it together."

They knelt by the bed. The cat jumped onto the bed and settled
in among the pillows. Then Florence kissed Arthur and tenderly
picked up the cat.

The boy was disgusted, terrified at the thought that the gray hairs that shone against the sheets' whiteness would creep into his mouth and slither down his lungs. *That cat is horrible. I don't know why Aunt Florence loves it.*

"Did you give her something?" Rafael asked.

"Are you crazy? She just got sick. She doesn't want to eat, and she screeches all the time. My aunt thinks a car hit her or one of the neighbors poisoned her."

They watched the darkness grow as they sat in the park. Arthur drew figures in the dirt with the end of the branch. Suddenly Rafael exclaimed, "Look, a four-leaf clover!"

"No, it's not. It's got five."

"Darn! I thought it was a good-luck charm."

"Hey, why don't you come over to my house? I want to show you my bullfighters' album."

"You sure your aunt won't get mad?"

"She's so sad about the cat, she won't even know you're there."

From the corner, the children could see Florence waiting at the front door. She came up to Arthur, put her hand on his head, and caressed his black hair.

"You're going to have to do me a favor," she said in tears. "There's no hope for the kitty. I spoke to the doctor about putting her to sleep. It's the only way to avoid her suffering. I couldn't bear to bring her there myself. Here's the address. Say you've come for me and give them the cat and the twenty pesos. And hurry back. Don't wait around and watch how they do it."

They went into the house. The cat sat motionless in an armchair. After smothering it with tears and kisses, Florence picked it up and placed it in a straw basket lined with cotton. As she watched the children depart, she was unable to hold back her sobs.

"How much did she give you?" Rafael asked when they had gotten to the next block.

"Twenty pesos. Didn't you hear?"

"Wow! So much money just to kill a cat?"

"I guess that's what it costs."

"You want to know what I just thought of?"

"No, what? Tell me."

"We could just let the cat go somewhere and keep the money."

"No way! Can you imagine what my aunt would say if it got better and came back home? It was lost once for a long time and then came back. That could happen again."

"So we'll kill it."

"No, I'd be too scared."

"Scared of what? You think it's so hard?"

"If my aunt ever found out . . ."

"She'll never know. Don't be an idiot. Twenty pesos. Twenty whole pesos!"

They kept walking along the street instead of getting on the bus. Arthur touched the breathing animal all curled up between the cotton and the straw. (The cat . . . the little dead kittens . . . the white mouse's blood . . . *My aunt loved her more than she loved me* . . .)

"And what are we going to do with all that money?"

"Tons of stuff. We could buy model airplanes."

"I've never put together a model airplane."

"Well, it's also enough to go to two movies, rent bicycles, buy candy, buy fishing hooks, and go row-boating in Chapultepec."

"Yeah, but how're we going to kill her?"

"There's lots of traffic here. Just close the basket and throw it into the street. No one will see anything."

"No. She'll suffer too much. Once I saw a dog . . ."

"You're right. Let's think of something else."

"Why not just give her to somebody?"

"What a dummy! Who'd want her? But listen. Why don't we throw her into the water?"

"I think cats know how to swim."

"Look. Let's go to the park. There's nobody there at this time of day, and once we're there we'll figure something out."

It can't be thought Arthur, trying to control the blood pulsating through his veins, the chill that was creeping up his vertebrae, *Rafael feels nothing—I can't be scared.*

The park was deserted. Dampness seemed to spring from the reservoir and cling to the trees. Rafael jumped up to grab onto the lowest branches and swing to and fro.

"We can hang her."

"She'll suffer too much," Arthur repeated. He wanted to caress the cat but was stopped short by a miaow as it squirmed inside its prison.

"She's going to escape," Rafael warned.

"No way. Can you imagine if that happened?"

"Come on then. We've got to do something."

Arthur rubbed his hands together and shivered from the cold. The moon shed eerie shadows around them. Rafael found a concrete slab. He bent down and picked it up.

"Hold onto the cat, and I'll throw this at her."

"Isn't there any other way?"

"No. Just do as I tell you."

Arthur picked up the cat and held it around the stomach.

"Hurry up. This is real heavy."

"Go ahead. Just don't hit me."

Rafael held the slab and kept it poised for a few seconds.

"I'll count to three, then throw it. Ready. One . . . two . . ."

The cat sensed the danger. It's body suddenly regained its flexibility and, escaping from Arthur's grasp, it jumped, landed two yards away, and disappeared into the bushes.

"What a jerk you are! You let her go!"

"I couldn't hold onto her. I don't know how she got away."

Rafael dropped the slab and sat down on the ground. Arthur was petrified. A minute later he began talking.

"We've got to go look for her. She's alive, and she's going to make her way back home."

"Now we really blew it. Call her and see if she'll come."

"Do you think she will?"

He did not know how long they looked for her, crawled through the bushes, dug into every corner of the park, called to her only to be heard by crickets, frogs, birds: the other sounds of the night that shielded the cat.

Exhausted and frightened, Arthur said good-bye to Rafael. He walked home with the fear of finding the cat in the armchair as always (the soft, elastic, immortal cat with nine gray lives).

Florence was playing cards when Arthur arrived. The boy explained that there were a lot of people at the veterinarian's office and he had been the last to be called. Florence attributed Arthur's upset to the disagreeable nature of the task she had given him to do, one she should have done herself.

Dawn found him awake, sleepless, drenched in sweat under the twisted sheets. Every little sound seemed to be the cat's step. He stood up, grabbed the twenty-peso bill, and tore it to pieces in front of the window. The wind dispersed the little bits of paper but did not rid him of the fear. He sat on the edge of the bed and tried to dream or to wake up from the dream . . . In the other room,

Florence opened her eyes and searched by her side for the imprint of another's weight, of the soft, firm body she used to polish with caresses: slow, useless caresses that spent her, helped her to forget the days.

THE CAPTIVE

At six o'clock in the morning an earthquake shook the entire town from top to bottom. We ran out into the streets fearing that the houses were going to topple down on top of us. And once we were outside, we were afraid the ground would open up under our feet.

The quake was over, but the women continued to pray. A few alarmists said that there would soon be another one of greater intensity. The general anxiety was so great, we thought they would not send us off to school. Classes began an hour late. In class, we all spoke about our experiences during the cataclysm, until the professor said that at our age, fourth-graders that we were, we should not be superstitious like the rest of the people in the town, nor should we ascribe the cause of natural phenomena to divine judgments or omens or the unleashing of evil forces. And in any case, the quake had caused no catastrophes: the only buildings that sustained any real damage were the colonial churches and houses.

We were convinced by his arguments and repeated them, more or less faithfully, to our parents. By the afternoon, everything had returned to normal. Sergio and Guillermo stopped by the house to get me. We went out into the lush field between the river and the cemetery. The setting sun reflected off the marble crosses and the granite monuments.

Guillermo suggested we go have a look at what had happened

to the ruins of the convent that stood near town. We were usually afraid to go there after dark; but that afternoon everything seemed fascinating and explainable.

We walked past the cemetery and, choosing the most difficult path, we climbed up the hill until it became so steep we almost had to crawl along on our bellies. We felt dizzy when we looked down but, without uttering a word, each of us was trying to prove that the other two were the cowards.

We finally reached the ruins of the convent that rose up at the top of the hill. We walked through the portico. We stopped in front of the wall that surrounded the terrace and the first cells. We found some dead bees on the floor tiles. Guillermo went over and picked one up. Silently, he came back and joined us. We walked through a hallway where the humidity and the nitrate had corroded the ancient frescoes.

Without confessing to each other our growing fears, we found our way to the cloister, which was even more ravaged than the other parts of the building. The central patio was covered with thistles and weeds. Two rotten beams leaned against a cracked wall.

We climbed a broken staircase to the second floor. Darkness had set in, and it was beginning to rain. The first sounds of the night rose all around us. The rain resounded on the porous stones. The wind sighed in the darkness.

As he approached the window, Sergio saw, or thought he saw, in what had been the cemetery, balls of fire zigzagging through the broken crosses. We heard a thunderclap. A bat flew off the ceiling. The flapping of its wings echoed dully against the dome.

We ran down the hallway and were nearing the door to the staircase when we heard Sergio scream: his whole body was shaking, and he just barely managed to point to one of the cells. We grabbed him by his arms and, without hiding our fears any longer, went toward the cell. As we were about to enter, Sergio pried himself loose, ran through the hallway, and left us there alone.

We soon realized that a wall had fallen and, full of terror, we looked into what had been a crypt or perhaps an ossarium: pieces of coffins, disintegrated bones, skulls.

Suddenly, in the semidarkness, we saw the white tunic of a woman who was seated on an iron chair. A mummified body: intact in its infinite calm and perpetual immobility.

I felt the cold rush of fear through every vein and joint. I summoned up all my strength and approached the cadaver. With three fingers I touched the forehead's wrinkled skin: under the slightest pressure the body disintegrated, turning to dust on the metal chair. It seemed as if the entire world was falling to pieces along with the captive in the convent. Everything swam before my eyes; the night was filled with a clamor and uproar, and the walls crumbled and were laid to waste as their secret was revealed.

Guillermo then dragged me out of the cell and, heedless of danger, we dashed down the hill at full speed. At the entrance to town, we met up with the men Sergio had called to help us. They went up to the convent. When they returned, they ascertained that indeed it was a crypt from around 1800 with some pulverized remains from that period. There was no cadaver. That had been an hallucination, a product of our fear, the storm and the darkness that caught us unawares in the ruins, a delayed reaction to the shock the earthquake had produced in the whole town.

I could not sleep. My parents stayed near me. During the following days, the only person among all of those who questioned us who gave any credence to our story was the priest. He told of a legendary crime recorded in the annals of our town, a monstrous revenge that was carried out at the end of the eighteenth century but which nobody could prove had occurred until then. The cadaver that had dissolved under my touch was that of a woman who had been given a paralyzing potion and who, when she came to her senses, found herself walled into a tenebrous crypt accompanied only by cadavers and unable to get up from the chair in which we found her nearly two hundred years later.

Time passed. I have not returned to the town, nor have I seen Sergio and Guillermo again, but each earthquake fills me with panic, for I feel as if the earth will spew up its bodies and only my hand will let them rest: the other death.

AUGUST AFTERNOON

You will never forget that August afternoon. You were fourteen years old and in your last year of junior high school. Your father had died before you could remember; your mother worked in a travel agency. She always woke you up at seven o'clock. You would leave behind a dream of battles along the coast, disembarkments on enemy islands, attacks on jungle forts. And you would slowly enter the day, therein to live, eat breakfast, go to school, grow up, painfully grow up, abandon your childhood.

At night, when your mother returned from the agency, you would eat dinner together in silence, and then you would close yourself up in your room to study, listen to the radio, read novels from the Bazooka collection: stories about World War Two through which you experienced a heroic era replete with silent battles without defeat.

Because of your mother's work, you always ate lunch at her brother's house. He was a surly man who never showed you any affection and demanded monthly payments for feeding you. Every day you had to put up with an aridity you never bargained for, a conversation that freed you, by excluding you, from having to talk about the same topics again and again, from having to repeat sen-

67

tences and postures gleaned from movies and television. Forced to accept you, they made no effort to relieve the discomfort of the involuntary intruder.

Nevertheless, Julia's presence compensated for everything. Julia, your first cousin, your unattainable first cousin who turned twenty that August afternoon. Julia studied chemistry and was the only one who paid any attention to you, but not out of love as you then imagined. Perhaps she felt pity for a child, an orphan who had no rights at all.

Julia helped you with your homework, she let you listen to her twenty records, music that will always make you think of her. One time, Julia took you to the movies; another, she introduced you to her boyfriend, the first of her boyfriends who was allowed to visit her at home.

And you never hated anyone as much as you hated Pedro—Pedro, who was irritated by your cousin's compassion for you; Pedro, who thought of you as a witness, a pest, perhaps never as a rival.

Julia turned twenty that August afternoon. After the birthday lunch was over, Pedro invited her to go to the movies or drive around the outskirts of the city. You did not hear her response. But you did obey the order to accompany them. You got into Pedro's car. You sank deep down into the back seat.

And Julia leaned her head on Pedro's shoulder while Pedro steered with his left hand so he could embrace Julia, and the music vibrated on the radio, the afternoon sizzled away in that city of stones and dust,

until you saw the last houses and the barracks and the cemeteries disappear from the window. Then (Julia kissed Pedro and let him caress her; blinded by the sun, you did not exist) cypresses, *oyameles*, and tall pine trees fragmented by the summer light came before your eyes and stopped you from crying.

Pedro parked the car in front of the walls of the convent hidden in the mountain's desolation. They asked if you wanted to get out, and the three of you walked through deserted corridors, hallways full of echoes without memory,

and they found a staircase that led down to a dark basement, and they talked to each other and listened (they, not you) to the acoustics of the chapel walls, and while Julia and Pedro rambled through the gardens of the convent, you—who do not have a name and are nobody—scrawled her name and the date on the walls.

They left the ruins and walked toward the humid jungle and the mountainous vegetation. They descended to where the forest is born, to the cold stream that was smaller than a ridge between furrows, all the way to the sign that read don't cut the flowers or disturb the animals (the jungle was a national park and offenders would be fined and imprisoned and humiliated without mercy).

The sharp, free air came to you and revived your dreams. You touched nature's freedom and thought you were a hero, all the heroes of the last war, the vanquishers and the vanquished at Tobruk, Narvik, Dunkirk, Ardennes, Iwo Jima, Midway, Monte Cassino, El Alamein, Warsaw,

you saw yourself fighting in the Afrika Korps or with the Polish Mounted Guards in suicide attacks against German tanks; you, a soldier capable of every and any warlike action because he knows that a woman is going to celebrate his deed and the enemy is going to lose, surrender, die.

And then Julia found the squirrel, the gray squirrel at the top of the tree, and she said how much she would like to bring it home, and Pedro answered that squirrels never let themselves be caught, and there were a hundred, a thousand, a hundred thousand rangers to protect the park and the squirrels. Then you said I'll get it,

and you climbed the tree before Julia could say no. (The pine bark cut your hands; you slipped on the resin.) Then the squirrel climbed to the highest point in the tree, and you followed it until you were standing out on a single branch. You looked down and saw the park ranger approaching and Pedro beginning to talk to him and Julia trying not to look at you,

but nevertheless she saw you, and Pedro did not say anything about you to the ranger, and the ranger did not look up, and Pedro kept talking to him, thus prolonging your humiliation,

your broken victory,

because ten minutes had already gone by and the branch was beginning to give.

You were afraid of falling and dying and failing in front of Julia, and losing face in front of her because the ranger was going to arrest you,

wounded and arrested and defeated in front of Julia,

nevertheless the ranger did not leave, and the squirrel teased you from just a half a yard away and scurried down and ran across the grass and disappeared into the jungle,

while Julia cried, far from the ranger and the squirrel, but further still from you and impossible.

And the ranger said good-bye to Pedro and finally you could come down from the tree,

pale, awkward, humiliated, in tears,

nevertheless Pedro laughed and Julia did not cry: she criticized him and called him stupid.

They got into the car again, and Julia did not let Pedro embrace her, and nobody said a word about anything.

You got out near your house and walked for hours and told your mother what had happened in the forest,

the end of your adventure and your painful innocence.

And you burned your Bazooka collection

and you never forgot that August afternoon,
that afternoon,
the last
in which you saw Julia.

ACHERON

It is five in the afternoon, the rain has stopped. Sunday, buried under a damp light, seems momentarily empty. The girl enters the café. Two elderly couples and a father with four small children observe her. She quickly and shyly crosses the room and sits down to the extreme left.

For only one moment, the sun's brilliant silhouette can be seen against the windows. The waiter approaches, she orders a lemonade, takes out a pad of paper, and begins to write on its pages. Squeaky old music comes over the speakers, background music that will not drown out the conversations (as it happens, there are no conversations).

The waiter serves the lemonade, she thanks him, puts some sugar in the tall glass, and stirs it with the metal spoon. She tastes the sweet-sour drink, then turns her attention back to what she is writing with her red pen. A letter? a poem? homework? a diary? a story? It is impossible to know, just as it is impossible to know why she is alone and with nowhere to go on a Sunday afternoon. She might also be ageless: she could be fourteen as well as eighteen or twenty. There is something that makes her exceptionally attractive: the harmonious fragility of her body, the long, brown hair, the subtly slanted eyes. Or perhaps it is her air of innocence and helplessness or the gravity of someone who carries a secret.

A young man of the same age or slightly older sits down somewhere on the terrace that is separated from the room by a pane of glass. He summons the waiter and orders coffee. Then he looks inside the room. His eyes sweep over empty spaces, silent groups of people, until they rest for a moment on the girl.

Feeling herself observed, she lifts her eyes, drops them, busies herself again with her writing. It is almost dark outside. The room floats in the half-light of the dusk until the glaring fluorescent lights are turned on. The gray hue dissipates into a fictitious daylight clarity.

She looks up again. Their eyes meet. She stirs her drink with her spoon. The sugar that has settled on the bottom dissolves in the lemonade. He tastes the coffee that is still too hot; immediately his gaze returns to the girl. He smiles when he sees that she is looking at him and then lowers his head. This hide and seek, this game that amuses and exalts them is repeated with slight variations for fifteen, twenty, twenty-five minutes. Finally he looks at her openly and smiles once again. She still tries to hide, conceal the fear, the desire, or the mystery that prevents a natural encounter.

The glass reflects her image, furtively mimics her movements, duplicates them without depth or perspective. Again it begins to rain; gusts of wind carry the water onto the terrace, wetting the boy's clothes as he begins to show signs of restlessness and a desire to leave.

Then she tears a sheet of paper from her pad, anxiously writes a few lines while glancing up at him. She taps the side of her glass with the spoon. The waiter approaches the table, listens to the girl's request, steps back, gestures, responds with indignation, and retreats haughtily.

The waiter's outburst is heard by everyone present. The girl blushes and does not know where to hide. The boy, paralyzed, watches the scene he cannot fathom because the logical outcome was quite different. Before he can intervene, overcome the shyness that always oppresses him when he finds himself in public alone, without the support, the incentive, the critical eyes of his friends, the girl rises, places some money on the table, and walks out of the café.

He watches her leave without attempting to move, then he reacts, taps on the window to ask for the bill. The waiter who refused to transmit the message goes over to the cash register. The young man anxiously waits two, three minutes, takes the bill, pays, steps out into the evening world darkened by rain. At the corner, where the streets branch, he looks in every direction into the depth of the Sunday city that will conceal the girl forever.

BATTLES IN THE DESERT

To the memory of Juan Manuel Torres
To Eduardo Mejia

The past is a foreign country. They do things differently there.
—L. P. Hartley, *The Go-Between*

I ﹠ The Ancient World

I remember, I don't remember. What year was it? We already had supermarkets, but still no television, only radio: *The Adventures of Charles LaCroix, Tarzan, The Lone Ranger, The Legion of the Dawn Treaders, The Child Professors, Tales from the Streets of Mexico, Panseco, Doctor I.Q., Doctor Lovesick from Her Soul Clinic*. Paco Malgesto narrated the bullfights; Carlos Albert covered soccer games; Mago Septién was the baseball announcer. The first postwar cars had begun to circulate: Packards, Cadillacs, Buicks, Chryslers, Mercurys, Hudsons, Pontiacs, Dodges, Plymouths, De Sotos. We went to see Errol Flynn and Tyrone Power movies, to matinees featuring an entire film from beginning to end. My favorite was *The Mongo Invasion*. The most popular songs of the day were "Without You," "La Rondalla," "My Little Donkey," "La Múcura," "My Little Love." Once again, an old Puerto Rican bolero could be heard everywhere: "However high the heavens or the skies, / however deep the ocean lies, / nothing in the world from you will keep / my love for you so true and deep."

It was the year of polio: the schools were full of children with orthopedic devices; the year of the foot-and-mouth-disease: tens of thousands of sick cattle were being shot throughout the country; the year of the floods: downtown had once again become a lake, and the people rode in boats through the streets. They say that with the next storm, the sewage system will burst and inundate the capital. So what, my brother answered, we are living up to our ears in shit anyway under Miguel Alemán's regime.

The face of El Señor Presidente was everywhere: immense drawings, idealized portraits, ubiquitous photographs, allegories of progress showing Miguel Alemán as Our Father Who Art in Heaven, laudatory caricatures, monuments. Public adulation, incessant private abuse. As punishment, we had to write in our notebooks a thousand times: I must obey, I must obey my parents and my teachers. They taught us national history, national language, geography of the capital city: the rivers (there were still rivers), the mountains (they were still visible). This was the ancient world. The grown-ups complained about inflation, exchange rates, traffic, immorality, noise, delinquency, overpopulation, beggars, foreigners, corruption, the limitless wealth of the few and the abject misery of almost everyone else.

The newspapers said: This is an anguished moment for the entire world. The specter of final war is hovering on the horizon. The atomic mushroom was the dismal symbol of our times. Nevertheless, there was still hope. Our textbooks confirmed this: Mexico, as can be seen on the map, is shaped like a cornucopia, a horn of plenty. For a still unimaginable 1980, a future of plenitude and universal well-being was predicted, without specifying just how it would be achieved. Clean cities without injustice, poor people, violence, congestion, or garbage. Every family with an ultramodern and aerodynamic (words from that era) house. No one will want for anything. Machines will do all the work. Streets full of trees and fountains, traveled by silent, nonpolluting vehicles that never collide. Paradise on earth. Finally, utopia will have been found.

In the meantime, we modernized and incorporated into our vocabulary terms that had sounded like Chicanoisms when we had first heard them in the Tin Tan movies and then slowly, imperceptibly, had become Mexicanized: *tenquíu, oquéi, uasamara, sherap, sorry, uan móment pliis.* We began to eat *hamburguesas, páys, donas, jotdogs, malteadas, áiscrim, margarina, pinutbuter.* Fresh juice drinks of lemon, jamaica, and sage were buried by Coca-Cola. Only the very poor continued to drink *tepache.* Our parents soon got used to drinking *jaibol,* even though at first it had tasted to them like medicine. Tequila is prohibited in my house, I once heard my Uncle Julian say. I serve only whisky to my guests: We must whitewash the taste of Mexicans.

II ◆§ Ravages of War

During recess we used to eat those kinds of cream tarts that no longer exist. We played in two gangs: Arabs and Jews. Israel had just been established and there was a war against the Arab League. The children who really were Jews and Arabs only insulted each other or fought when they spoke. Our professor, Bernardo Mondragón, said to them: You were born here. You are as Mexican as your fellow students. Don't pass on the hatred. After all that has happened (the endless massacres, the extermination camps, the atomic bomb, the millions and millions of deaths), the world of tomorrow, the world in which you will grow up and be men, should be a peaceful place, without crime, without vileness. A short laugh rang out from the back row. Mondragón watched us sadly, probably asking himself what will become of us over the years, how many evils and catastrophes are we yet to witness.

The extinguished brilliance of the Ottoman Empire still persisted like the light of a long-dead star. For me, a child of the Roman Quarter, both Jews and Arabs were "Turks." The "Turks" didn't seem as strange as Jim, who was born in San Francisco and spoke two languages without an accent; or Toru, who was brought up in a concentration camp for Japanese; or Peralta and Rosales. They did not pay tuition; they were on scholarship; they lived in the run-down neighborhood called the Doctors Quarter. The Highway of Piety—not yet renamed Cuauhtémoc Avenue—and Urueta Park formed the border line between the Roman Quarter and Doctors. Little Rome was another town altogether. The Bag Man lurks there. The Great Kidnapper. If you go to Little Rome, my son, they will kidnap you, scratch your eyes out, cut off your hands and your tongue, then throw you out into the streets to beg, and the Bag Man will take everything you get. During the day he is a beggar; at night he is an elegant millionaire, thanks to the exploitation of his victims. The fear of being near Little Rome. The fear of riding the streetcar over the Coyoacán Avenue bridge: only rails and girders. Underneath runs the dirty River of Piety, which sometimes overflows when it rains.

Before the war in the Middle East, our class's main sport revolved around giving Toru a hard time. Slant eyes, Chinaman, ate the shit and away he ran. Watch out, Toro, I'm going to nail you up by the horns. I never joined in with the jeers. I thought about how I would feel if I were the only Mexican in a school in Tokyo; about how Toru must suffer when he sees those movies that portray the Japanese as gesticulating monkeys who died by the thousands. Toru was the best student in the class. He excelled in every subject. Always studying, with a book in his hands. He knew jujitsu. One time he got sick of it and almost tore Domínguez to pieces. He forced him to get down on his hands and knees and beg for forgiveness. Nobody messed with Toru after that. Today he manages a Japanese factory and employs four thousand Mexican slaves.

I am from the Irgun. I will kill you: I am from the Arab League. The battles in the desert began. We called it that because it was a courtyard of red earth—brick and volcanic rock dust—without any plants or trees, just a cement box in the back. It was built over a passageway leading from the house on the corner to the street across the way that was used as an escape route during the times of religious persecution. We thought this underground area was a vestige of some prehistoric era. Nevertheless, the Cristero war was closer to us at that time than our infancy is to us now. This was the religious war against reform in which many members of my mother's family participated as more than just sympathizers. Twenty years later she continued to worship martyrs like Father Pro and Anacleto González Flores. No one, on the other hand, remembered the thousands of dead peasants, the agrarian reform advocates, the rural professors, the press gangs.

I did not understand anything: war, any war, seemed to me to be the stuff of which movies are made. Sooner or later the good guys win (who are the good guys?). Fortunately, there had been no wars in Mexico since General Cárdenas squelched the Saturnino Cedillo uprising. This was difficult for my parents to believe, because their childhood, adolescence, and youth were spent against a background of constant battles and executions. But things seemed to be going well that year. Classes were constantly being called off so they could take us to the inaugurations of highways, avenues, sports arenas, dams, hospitals, ministries, enormous buildings.

As a rule, they were nothing more than a pile of rocks. The president inaugurated enormous unfinished monuments to himself. Hours and hours under the sun without so much as a sip of water—hey, Rosales, bring some lemons, they're great to quench your thirst, pass one over here—waiting for Miguel Alemán to arrive. Young, smiling, simpatico, shining, waving from aboard a cattle truck surrounded by his retinue. Applause, confetti, paper streamers, flowers, girls, soldiers (still wearing their French helmets), gunmen, the eternal little old lady who breaks through the military barricade and is photographed with El Señor Presidente as she hands him a bouquet of roses.

I had many friends, but my parents did not like any of them:

Jorge because he was the son of a general who fought against the
Cristeros; Arturo because his parents were divorced and he was
looked after by an aunt who charged people to read their fortunes;
Alberto because his widowed mother worked in a travel agency, and
a decent woman should never work outside the home. That year
Jim and I became friends. During these inaugurations, which had
become a natural part of life, Jim would say: Today my father is
going to come. And then: Do you see him? He is the one with the
sky-blue tie. There he is, standing next to President Alemán. But
nobody could distinguish him from all those other heads plastered
with linseed oil or cream. But yes, they often published pictures of
him. Jim carried the clippings around in his knapsack. Did you see
my dad in *El Excélsior*? How strange: you don't look like him at
all. Well, they say I look like my mother. I'm going to look like
him when I grow up.

III ✑ Ali Baba and the Forty Thieves

It seemed strange for Jim, whose father was an influential businessman and held an important position in the government, to be attending a run-of-the-mill school more appropriate for those of us
who lived in the downwardly mobile Roman Quarter than for the
son of Miguel Alemán's omnipotent close friend and banking part-
ner. Every time the president blinked, Jim's father made millions:
contracts for everything; land in Acapulco; import-export and con-
struction permits; authorization to establish subsidiaries of North
American companies in Mexico; stocks in the asbestos industry just
when a new law was proclaimed requiring all porches to be lined
with carcinogenic asbestos; the reselling of powdered milk destined
for free school breakfasts in poor neighborhoods; falsification of
vaccinations and medicines; enormous dealings in gold and silver

on the black market; large parcels of land bought for pennies an acre just weeks before the announcement of a new round of development projects that would raise the value ten thousand times; a hundred million pesos changed into dollars and deposited in Switzerland the day before the devaluation.

Even less comprehensible was that Jim would live with his mother in an apartment on the third floor near the school rather than in a mansion in Las Lomas, or at least in Polanco. Strange . . . Not really, the others would say during recess. Jim's mother is that guy's *mistress*. His wife is an old hag who always appears at social events. If you want to see her, just watch where they're giving things away to poor children (ha, ha, my dad says that first they make them poor and then they give them handouts). She's obese and repulsive. She looks like a cross between a parrot and a mammoth. But Jim's mother, on the other hand, is young, beautiful. Some people think she is his sister. And, Ayala chimed in, he isn't the son of that son-of-a-thieving-bastard who's fucking Mexico over anyway. His father is a *gringo* journalist who took his mother with him to San Francisco and then wouldn't marry her. The Señor doesn't treat Jim very well. They say he's got women all over the place. Even movie stars and things like that. Jim's mother is just one of many.

That's not true, I answered. Don't talk like that. How would you like it if they talked about your mothers that way? No one dared say these things directly to Jim but, as if intuiting what they were saying, he insisted: I don't see my dad very much because he's always abroad, working for his country. Sure, whatever you say, Alcaraz replied: "Working for his country"—Ali Baba and the forty thieves. At home they say they're even stealing what isn't there to steal. The whole Alemán government is just a den of thieves. Why don't they buy you a new sweater with the money they steal from the rest of us?

Jim starts to fight and doesn't want to talk to anybody. I cannot imagine what would happen if he found out what they were saying about his mother behind his back (when Jim is present, our classmates limit their attacks to the Señor). Jim has become my friend because I do not judge him. In other words, it is not his fault. Nobody chooses how, when, where, or to whom one is born. We will no longer participate in the recess wars. Today the Jews took over Jerusalem, but tomorrow the Arabs will get their revenge.

After school on Fridays, Jim and I would often go to the Rome, the Royal, the Balmori: movie theaters that no longer exist. Lassie or young Elizabeth Taylor movies. And our favorite was the triple feature we must have seen a thousand times: *Frankenstein, Dracula,* and *The Wolfman.* Or the double feature: *Adventures in Burma* and *God Is My Co-Pilot.* Or even the one Father Pérez del Valle loved to show on Sundays in the Club Vanguard: *Goodbye, Mr. Chips.* It made me as sad as when I saw *Bambi.* I saw that Walt Disney movie when I was three or four, and they had to drag me out of the theater in tears because the hunters had killed Bambi's mother. They killed millions of mothers during the war. But I did not know that; I did not cry for them or their children, even though in Movieland—along with Donald Duck, Mickey Mouse, Popeye the Sailorman, Woody the Woodpecker, and Bugs Bunny cartoons— they showed the newsreels: bomb formations falling on cities, cannons, battles, fires, ruins, dead bodies.

IV ❧ A Middle Ground

I had so many brothers and sisters I could never invite Jim over to my house. My mother was always cleaning up after us, cooking, or washing clothes. She would have loved to buy a washing machine, a vacuum cleaner, a blender, a pressure cooker, an electric refrigerator (ours was one of the last existing iceboxes that needed to be loaded with a fresh block of ice every morning). At that time my mother could only see the narrow horizon she had been shown at home. She detested everyone who was not from Jalisco. She thought that all other Mexicans were foreigners and particularly loathed those from the capital. She hated the Roman Quarter because all the good families were beginning to move out and only Arabs, Jews, and Southerners—people from Campecho, Chiapas, Tabasco, Yucatán—were moving in. She scolded Hector who was already twenty years old, and instead of attending classes at the National University where he was enrolled, spent his days at the Swing Club and in pool halls, cantinas, and whorehouses. His greatest passion was to talk about women, politics, and automobiles. Everyone complains so much about the military, he would say, and just look at what happens to the country when they stick in a civilian president. If they had not cheated my dear General Henríquez Guzmán, Mexico would be in as good shape as Argentina is now with General Perón. You'll see, you'll see how things are going to be around here in 1952. I'll lay odds Henríquez Guzmán will be president, with the Revolutionary Party or against it.

My father spent all his time at his soap factory, which was rapidly going under due to the competition and marketing of the North American brands. The new detergents were being advertised over the radio: Ace, Fab, Vel, and they proclaimed that soap was a thing of the past. While for most of us (still ignorant of the dangers) all those suds meant cleanliness, comfort, well-being and, for women, a liberation from endless hours at the wash basin, they were, for my family, the crest of a wave that was sweeping away our privileges.

Monseigneur Martínez, the archbishop of Mexico, decreed one day of prayer and penance to halt the advance of communism. I will never forget that morning. During recess, while I was showing Jim one of my Big Little Books—those illustrated stories with tabs

in the upper corners of the pages that look like cartoons when you
thumb through them quickly—Rosales, who had never picked on
me before, shouted, Hey, look at those two faggots. Let's go beat
the shit out of those faggots. And he started to attack me. Your
mother's a whore. You son-of-a-bitch. Just you wait and see who's
a faggot, you fucking Indian. The teacher pulled us apart. I had a
split lip, and his nose was bleeding all over his shirt.

Thanks to that fight, my father taught me not to scorn others. He
asked me who I fought with. I said Rosales, that Indian. My father
said that in Mexico we are all Indians even if we do not know it or
want to be and that if the Indians were not poor, no one would consider it an insult. I called Rosales "trash." My father pointed out to
me that nobody is to blame for living in poverty and before judging
others I should ask myself if he has had the same opportunities as I.

Compared to Rosales I was a millionarie, but next to Harry
Atherton, I was a beggar. The previous year, when I was studying in
Mexico High School, Harry Atherton invited me over to his house
in Las Lomas: underground pool room, swimming pool, a library
with thousands of leather-bound volumes, a butler, wine cellars,
gymnasium, steam bath, tennis courts, six bathrooms (why do the
homes of wealthy Mexicans always have so many bathrooms?). His
room looked out onto a sloped garden with a waterfall and lots of
ancient trees. Harry had been sent to Mexico High School instead of
the American one so that he could be totally immersed in a Spanish-
speaking environment and thus familiarize himself with those people who would be his helpers, his eternal apprentices, his servants.

We ate dinner. His parents did not say a word to me and spoke
English throughout the entire meal. Honey, how do you like the
little spic? He's a midget, don't you think? Oh Jack, please. Maybe
the poor kid is catching on. Don't worry, dear, he won't understand
a thing. The next day, Harry said to me: I'm going to give you
some advice. Learn how to use your silverware. Last night you ate

your filet with your fish fork. And don't make so much noise with
your soup, don't talk with your mouth full, chew slowly, and take
small bites.

The exact opposite happened with Rosales right after I came to
this school, when the problems at my father's factory had already
made it impossible for him to pay the tuition at Mexico High
School. I went to Rosales's house to copy some civics notes from
him. He was an excellent student, the best in composition and spelling, and we all took advantage of him for things of this sort. He
lived in a neighborhood constructed out of boards. The broken pipes
inundated the patio. Shit floated in the greenish water.

His twenty-seven-year-old mother looked like she was fifty. She
was very friendly to me and, although I had not been invited, they
shared their dinner with me. Brain tacos. They made me sick. A
strange grease similar to car oil oozed out of them. Rosales slept on
a straw mat in the living room. His mother's new lover had ban-
ished him from the only bedroom.

V ᴥ However Deep the Ocean Lies

After the fight with Rosales, Jim was convinced that I was his
friend. One Friday, he did something he had never done before: he
invited me to his house for an after-school snack. I was sorry I
couldn't invited him over to mine. We walked up to the fourth floor
and opened the door. I have a key because my mother doesn't like
to keep a maid. The apartment smelled of perfume; it was tidy and
very clean. Garish furniture from Sears Roebuck. A picture portrait
of his mother by Semo Studios, another picture of Jim on his first
birthday (the Golden Gate Bridge in the background), many more
of the Señor on the Olive Train, in the presidential airplane, in
group photos. "The Cub of the Revolution" and his team. The first

university graduates to govern the country. Technicians, not politicians. Impeccable moral fiber, the propaganda insisted.

I never thought Jim's mother was going to be so young, so elegant, and above all, so beautiful. I did not know what to say to her. It is impossible to describe how I felt when she gave me her hand. I would have liked to just stand there staring at her. Please, go on into Jim's room. I'll finish preparing your snack. Jim showed me his collection of atomic pens (fountain pens that smelled awful, leaked sticky ink, and were all the rage that year when, for the last time, we used ink wells and blotters); toys the Señor had bought for him in the United States: missile-shooting cannons, jet-propulsion fighter bombers, soldiers armed with flamethrowers, plastic machine guns (plastics were just coming out), a Lionel electric train, a portable radio. I don't bring any of these things to school because nobody in Mexico has toys like this. No, of course not. We, the children of World War Two, had no toys. Everything went into war production. I read in *Reader's Digest* that even Parker and Esterbrook were manufacturing war materials. But I could not have cared less about the toys. Hey, what did you say your mother's name was? Mariana. That's what I call her. I don't call her Mom. What about you? Well, no. I address my mother formally, just like she does my grandmother. Don't make fun of me, Jim. Don't laugh.

Come have a bite to eat, Mariana said. And we sat down. I sat in front of her, looking at her. I did not know which to do: eat nothing or gobble everything down to make her feel good. If I eat, she'll think I'm a starving child; if I don't eat, she'll think I don't like her cooking. Chew slowly. Don't talk with your mouth full. What can we talk about? Fortunately, Mariana breaks the silence. How do you like them? They're called Flying Saucers. I toast them in this machine. I love them, ma'am; I've never eaten anything so delicious. Wonder Bread, ham, Kraft cheese, bacon, butter, ketchup, mayonnaise, mustard. It was all so different from the pozole, birria, tostadas, chicharron en salsa verde my mother made. Do you want another Flying Saucer? I would be more than happy to make one for you. No, thank you anyway, ma'am. They're delicious, but really, please don't bother.

She didn't touch a thing. She talked, she talked to me the whole time. Jim remained silent while he ate one Flying Saucer after another. Mariana asked me: What does your father do? I was ashamed to answer: He owns a factory that makes bath and laundry soap. The new detergents are putting him out of business. Oh, no. I'd never thought about it in that way. Pause. Silence. How many brothers and sisters do you have? Three sisters and a brother. Were you all born here in Mexico City? Only me and the youngest girl, and the rest were born in Guadalajara. We had a big house on San Francisco Street. They tore it down. Do you like school? School's not bad, but our classmates are the pits, don't you think, Jim?

Well, ma'am, if you will please excuse me, I have to go now (how can I explain to her that they'll kill me if I get home after eight?). Thanks a lot, ma'am. Everything was really delicious. I'm going to tell my mother to buy one of those toasters and make me some Flying Saucers. There aren't any in Mexico, Jim interjected, speaking up for the first time. If you want, I'll bring one back for you from the United States when I go.

You are always welcome here. Come back soon. Thank you very much again, ma'am. Thanks Jim. See you on Monday. How I would have loved to remain there forever or, at the very least, take along with me the photograph of Mariana that was in the living room. I walked down Tabasco Street, turned onto Córdoba to get to my house on Zacatecas. The silvery streetlamps only dimly illuminated the streets. A city immersed in semidarkness: the mysterious Roman Quarter of those days. An atom in the immense world, prepared many years before my birth like a stage set for my performance. I heard a bolero playing on a jukebox. Until that time, the only music we had heard was the National Anthem, church hymns, Cri-Cri and his children's songs: "Little Horses," "Parade of Letters," "Little Black Watermelon Boy," "The Cowboy Mouse," "Juan Pestañas," and that circular, dense, absorbing melody by Ravel that Radio XEQ played before beginning its daily broadcast at six-thirty in the morning when my father turned on the radio to wake me up to the clamor of the *Legion of the Dawn Treaders*. When I heard this other bolero that had nothing whatsoever to do with Ravel's, the words caught my attention. "However high the heavens or the skies, / however deep the ocean lies."

I looked down Álvaro Obregón Avenue and said to myself: I'm going to keep my memory of this moment intact because everything that now exists will never be the same again. One day it will all seem to have been part of the most remote prehistoric era. I'm going to preserve it because today I fell in love with Mariana. What will happen? Nothing will happen. Nothing could possibly happen. What will I do? Change schools so as not to see Jim anymore and therefore not see Mariana? Look for a girl my own age? But at my age, nobody can look for a girl. The only thing a person of my age can do is fall in love secretly, silently, like I had done with Mariana. Fall in love knowing that all is lost and there is no hope.

VI ᔐ Obsession

You're late. But Mom, I told you I was going to go to Jim's house for a snack. That's right, but nobody gave you permission to stay out until this time of night: it's eight-thirty. I was very very worried about you: I thought you had been killed or the Bag Man had kidnapped you. What kind of garbage did you eat? I wonder who *your little friend's* parents are. Is he the same one you go to the movies with?

Yes. His father is very important. He works for the government. For the government? And they live in that filthy building? Why didn't you ever tell me? What did you say his name was? Impossible: I know his wife. She and Aunt Elena are intimate friends. They don't have any children. It is a great tragedy in the midst of all that wealth and power. They're putting one over on you, Carlitos. I don't know why, but they sure are putting one over on you. I'm going to ask your teacher and get to the bottom of this mystery. No, please, I beg of you: don't say anything to Mondragón. What would Jim's mother think if she found out? She was very kind to me. Oh no, this is all I needed! What kind of secrets are you hiding? Okay, tell me the truth: you didn't really go over to this so-called Jim's house, did you?

I finally convinced my mother. In any case, she was left with the suspicion that something strange had occurred. I spent a very sad weekend. I became a child again and went to Ajusco Square to play alone with my little wooden cars. Ajusco Square is where they took me for sunbaths when I was a baby and where I learned to walk. Houses from the era of Porfirio Díaz, some that have already been demolished to make room for horrible buildings. The fountain in the shape of a figure eight; dead insects floating on the water. And Madame Sara P. de Madero lived between my house and the park. It seemed unbelievable to me that I could see, even from afar, a person whose name appeared in the history books, a participant in events that had occurred forty years earlier. That fragile, dignified old woman, still in mourning for her assassinated husband.

As I was playing in Ajusco Square, one part of me reasoned: how can you fall in love with Mariana if you've only seen her once and she's old enough to be your mother? It's stupid and ridiculous because there is not even a remote possibility that she'll feel something for you in return. But the other part of me, the stronger part, was deaf to all reasoning: I kept repeating her name as if the act of enunciating it again and again would bring her closer to me. Monday was even worse. Jim said: Mariana really liked you. She's glad we're friends. I thought: so she knows I exist, she noticed me, she realized—just a bit, at least a bit—the effect she had on me.

For weeks I asked about her, obliquely, using any pretext I could think of so as not to arouse Jim's suspicions. I tried to camouflage my interest while finding out everything I could about Mariana. Jim never told me anything I did not already know. He appeared to be totally ignorant of his own history. I wondered how it could be that everybody else was not. Again and again I begged him to take me to his house to see his toys, his illustrated books, his comics. Jim read comic books in English that Mariana bought for him at Sanborn's. He made fun of our heroes: Pepín, Paquín, Chamaco, Caron, and for the most privileged among us, Billiken, the Argentinian, and Peneca, the Chilean.

Since we always had a lot of homework, Friday was the only day of the week I could go over to Jim's house. At that time of day, Mariana was invariably at the beauty salon, getting ready for her evening out with the Señor. She would always return at eight-thirty or nine o'clock, and I could never wait until then to see her. Our snacks were always ready and waiting for us in the refrigerator: chicken salad, cole slaw, cold cuts, apple pie. Once, when Jim opened a closet, a picture of Mariana at six months old lying naked on a tiger-skin rug fell onto the floor. I felt a great wave of tenderness come over me when I thought about something one never thinks about because it is so obvious: Mariana had also been a little girl, she had been my age, and she would be a woman my mother's age and then an old lady like my grandmother. But at that moment she was the most beautiful woman in the world and I thought about her constantly. Mariana had become my obsession. However high the heavens or the skies, / however deep the ocean lies.

VII ⋑ Today Is the Day

And then one day—one of those cloudy days I love and nobody else
can stand—I could no longer control myself. We were in National
Language Class, as they used to call Spanish. Mondragón was teach-
ing us the past conditional: *Hubiera o hubiese amado, hubiéramos
o hubiésemos amado, hubierais o hubieseis amado, hubieran o
hubiesan amado.* It was eleven o'clock. I asked for permission to
go to the bathroom. Then I sneaked out of school. I rang the doorbell to Apartment 4. One, two, three times. Mariana finally came
to the door: fresh, beautiful, without any make-up. She was wearing
a silk kimono. She was holding a razor just like the one my father
used, only in miniature. She had been shaving her legs or her under-
arms when I rang the bell. She was, of course, surprised to see me.
Carlos, what are you doing here? Did something happen to Jim?
No, ma'am. Jim is just fine. Nothing happened.

Somehow we were already sitting on the sofa. Mariana crossed
her legs. For a split second her kimono opened ever so slightly. Her
knees, her thighs, her breasts, her flat belly, her mysterious hidden
sex . . . I don't know how to tell you this, ma'am. I'm very embarrassed. What are you going to think of me? Carlos, I really don't
understand. This is very strange to see you here like this at this
time of day. You should be in class, shouldn't you? Yes, of course,
it's just that I couldn't stand it any longer. I can't stand it. I ran
away from school without permission. If I get caught, they'll expel
me. Nobody knows I am here with you. Please, don't tell anybody
I came here. Don't tell Jim. I beg you, least of all Jim. Promise me
you won't.

Wait a minute. Calm down and let's see what this is all about.
Why are you so worked up? Did something terrible happen at

home? Are you having problems at school? Do you want some
chocolate milk, Coca-Cola, a sip of mineral water? Trust me. Tell
me how I can help you. No, you can't help me, ma'am. Why not,
Carlitos? Because I came to tell you—I'll just come out and say it
once and for all, please forgive me, ma'am—that I'm in love with
you.

I thought she was going to laugh, scream at me, tell me I was
crazy. Or maybe, better yet: Get out of here right now. I'm going
to tell your parents and your teacher. I dreaded all of these possible
reactions: all the ones I could have expected. Nevertheless, Mariana
was not outraged, and she did not make fun of me. She sat there
looking at me sadly. She took my hand (I'll never forget that she
took my hand) and said:

I understand you perfectly. You have no way of knowing how
well. Now you have to try to understand me and face the fact that
you are a child just like my son and, for you, I am an old lady: I
just turned twenty-eight years old. So, not now and not ever will
there be anything between us. You understand me, don't you? I
don't want you to suffer. Many terrible things await you in the future, you poor boy. Carlos, try to think of this as a joke, like something funny, so when you remember this as an adult, you will smile
and not feel any resestment about it. Keep coming here with Jim
and treat me just as what I am to you: your best friend's mother.
Don't stop coming over; act as if nothing has happened, and in this
way the *infatuation*—I'm sorry, love—will die down, and it won't
become a problem for you, a tragedy that could cause you lasting
damage for your entire life.

I felt like crying. But I controlled myself and said: You're right,
ma'am. I understand everything you say. I want to thank you very
much for reacting the way you did. Forgive me. In any case, I had
to tell you. I thought I would die if I didn't tell you. There is nothing to forgive you for, Carlos. I like it that you are honest and con-

front your feelings. Please don't tell Jim. I won't say a word. You needn't worry.

I freed my hand from hers. I got up to go. Then Mariana stopped me. Before you go, can I ask you for a favor? Let me give you a kiss. And she gave me a kiss, not exactly on the lips, but on the corner of my mouth. A kiss just like the ones Jim always got before going off to school. I was shaking. I did not kiss her. I said nothing. I went running down the stairs. Instead of going back to class, I walked all the way to Insurgentes Boulevard. I arrived home totally confused. I pretended I was sick and wanted to go to bed.

But the teacher had just called. Surprised at my sudden disappearance, they had looked for me in the bathrooms and throughout the entire school. Jim declared: He probably went to see my mother. At this time of day? Yeah, Carlos is real weird. You never know what's going on in his head. I think he's got a screw loose somewhere. He has a brother who's a half-crazy gangster.

Mondragón and Jim went to the apartment. Mariana confessed that I had been there for a few minutes to pick up my history book I had left there the Friday before. This lie made Jim furious. I don't know how, but he had figured out the whole thing and explained it in full detail to the teacher. Mondragón called the factory and the house to tell my family what I had done, even though Mariana had flatly denied everything. Her denial made me appear even more suspect in the eyes of Jim, Mondragón, and my parents.

VIII ◆§ The Prince of This World

I never dreamt you could be such a monster. You couldn't possibly have learned that kind of behavior in this house! Tell me the truth: it was Hector who led you into this foolishness. Anyone who corrupts minors deserves a slow, painful death and all of hell's worst punishments. Come on, speak up, don't just sit there crying like a sissy. Tell me that it was your brother who talked you into doing it.

Listen, Mother, I don't think I did anything so terrible. And you still have the gall to insist you haven't done anything wrong? As soon as your fever drops you are going to confess and take communion so that Our Lord Jesus Christ can forgive you your sins.

My father did not even scold me. He simply stated: This boy is abnormal. Something in his head just isn't working right. It must be from that fall on his head in Ajusco Square when he was six months old. I'm going to take him to see a specialist.

We are all hypocrites. We cannot see ourselves or judge ourselves the way we see and judge others. Even I, who never knew anything about what was going on, realized that for years my father had been maintaining another household: a woman—his ex-secretary—and two children. I remember an incident that occurred at the barbershop while I was waiting to get my hair cut. Some copies of *Vea* and *Vodevil* were lying next to the news magazines. I took advantage of the fact that the barber and his customer were engaged in exchanging verbal assaults against the government. I hid *Vea* inside *Hoy* and began leafing through the pages with pictures of Tongolele, Su Muy Key, Kalantán, all half-naked. Legs, breasts, mouths, waists, buttocks, the mysterious hidden sex.

The barber, who shaved my father almost every day and had been cutting my hair ever since I was a year old, could see my facial expressions through the mirror. Put that down, Carlitos. Those things are for grown-ups. I'm going to tell your father on you. That's when I figured out that children are not supposed to like women. And if you challenge this edict, they create an enormous scandal and tell you that you're crazy. How unfair!

When, I asked myself, was the first time I was conscious of feeling desire? Perhaps it was the previous year when I saw Jennifer Jones's naked shoulder in *Duel in the Sun* at the Chapultapec Theater. Or maybe it was when Antonia lifted up her skirt to mop the yellow-painted floor and I saw her legs. Antonia was very pretty and she was always kind to me. Nevertheless, once I said to her: You're bad because you kill chickens. It would upset me greatly to watch them die. Better to buy them already dead and plucked. But none of that lasted very long. Antonia left the house because Hector refused to leave her alone.

I did not return to school, and they prohibited me from going out anywhere else. They took me to Our Lady of Rosario Church where we attended Mass every Sunday, where I had done my first Holy Communion, and where, thanks to my steady attendance of Mass on the first Fridays of the month, I had accumulated some indulgences. My mother sat down on one of the benches, praying for my soul that was in danger of eternal damnation. I knelt down in front of the confessional. Scared to death, I told Father Ferrán everything.

In a soft and slightly panting voice, Father Ferrán questioned me on all the details: Was she naked? Was there a man in the house? Do you think she had committed a shameful act before opening the door? And then: Have you ever abused yourself? Have you ever brought on an ejaculation? I don't understand what you are talking about, Father. He then proceeded to give me an explicit description. When he realized that he was talking to a child who was as yet incapable of even producing the raw material necessary for an ejaculation, he regretted having done so and then launched off on a lecture I did not understand at all: as a result of our state of original sin, the devil is the prince of this world, and he is continually setting traps for us, attempting to lure us away from our love of the Lord and tempting us into sin: one more thorn in the crown of our Lord Jesus Christ.

I said: Yes, Father; but somehow I could not conceive of why the devil would personally bother about leading me into temptation. Even less so could I understand why Christ would suffer because I had fallen in love with Mariana. As is expected under the circumstances, I showed myself ready and willing to mend my ways. But I did not regret anything, and I did not feel guilty: to love someone is not a sin. Love is good; only hatred is demonic. That afternoon, Father Ferrán's lecture made much less of an impression on me than did his practical guide to masturbation. When I got home, I felt a great longing to abuse myself and bring on an ejaculation. I did not do it. Instead, I recited twenty Our Fathers and fifty Hail Marys. I took communion the next day. In the evening, they took me to a psychiatrist's office with white walls and nickel-plated furniture.

IX ⚜ Mandatory English

A young man asked me some questions and wrote down everything I said on lined sheets of yellow paper. I did not know what to say. Since I was totally ignorant of his profession's vocabulary, it was impossible to find a way for us to communicate. He asked me questions about my sisters and my mother that had never even entered my head. Then they made me draw every member of my family and paint trees and houses. Next they gave me the Rorschach test (is there anyone who *doesn't* see monsters in those ink blots?) with numbers and geometric figures and questions I was supposed to answer. The questions were as silly as the answers I gave. "What I like most": to climb trees and scale the walls of old houses; lemon sherbet; rainy days; adventure movies; Salgari novels. No, better yet: to lie awake in bed. But my father always dragged me out of bed at six-thirty in the morning to do exercises, even on Saturdays and Sundays. "What I hate most": cruelty toward people and animals; violence; screaming and shouting; arrogance; the abusiveness of older brothers; arithmetic; the fact that some people have nothing to eat while others have everything; finding garlic cloves in rice or stew; that they trim trees or kill them; watching someone throw bread away.

The woman who gave me the last tests spoke to the man right there in front of me. They acted as if I were a piece of furniture. It is very clearly an Oedipal problem, Doctor. This child is intellectually deficient. He is overprotected and docile. A castrating mother is undoubtedly the primal injury. He went to see that woman, fully aware that he might find her with her lover. I'm sorry, Elisita, but I have reached opposite conclusions: the boy is extremely intelligent and unusually precocious, so much so that by the time he is fifteen, he may become a total idiot. His abnormal behavior stems from a situation of neglect, excessive discipline from both parents, and a strong inferiority complex. Don't forget that he is very short for his age and the youngest male child. Note, if you will, how he identifies with the victim: animals, trees that cannot defend themselves. He is looking for the affection that is lacking within the family unit.

I felt like shouting at them: You idiots, why don't you at least come to an agreement before carrying on with this nonsense in a language you don't even understand yourselves?! Why do you have to label everything? Why don't you just accept the fact that someone can fall in love? Haven't you ever fallen in love? But the man came over to me and said: You can go now, my friend. We'll send the test results to your dad.

My father was sitting solemnly in the waiting room surrounded by worn-out copies of *Life, Look, Holiday* and glowing proudly because he could read them all fluently. He had just passed, at the top of his class, an adult night course in intensive English, and he studied every day with workbooks and records. It was so strange to see a person of his age—an old man of forty-two!—studying. Very early every morning, after his exercises and before breakfast, he reviewed his irregular verbs: *be, was, were, been; have, had, had; get, got, gotten; break, broke, broken; forget, forgot, forgotten;* and he practiced his pronounciation: apple, world, country, people, business. These words came to Jim so naturally and yet were so difficult for my father.

Those were terrible weeks. Only Hector defended me. Wow, you sure got it on! You scored quite some number there. I mean, you start making it now with chicks like her, hot stuff, better than Rita Hayworth, and what won't you do when you grow up? Hey, man? You're all right: trying to catch some action now before you're really up to it, instead of jerking off. I'm sure glad that neither of us turned into faggots even with so many sisters. But watch your step, Carlitos; don't let that bastard set his goons on you and break your ass. But Hector, my God, it's not such a big deal. The only thing I did was tell her I was in love with her. There's nothing wrong with that. I didn't do anything else. Seriously, I don't understand what all the fuss is about.

You were bound to end up at a school for beggars what with your father's greediness, my mother insisted. He throws money away on *other* expenses, but when it comes to his own children, he never has any. Can you believe it: letting the son of a woman *like that* into the school? We must transfer you to a school for our kind of people, from our class. And Hector: But, Mom, what class are you talking about? We are right where we belong: a typical Roman Quarter family on the way down: the essence of the Mexican middle class. Carlos is just fine where he is. That school is precisely for people of our class. Where else are you going to put him?

X ◆§ Fire Rain

My mother always insisted that our family—that is to say, her family—was one of the best in Guadalajara. Never any scandals like the one I had created. Honorable, hard-working men. Devout women, self-sacrificing wives, exemplary mothers. Obedient and respectful children. Then came the Indian hordes seeking their revenge against decency and good blood. The revolution—the old chieftains, that is—confiscated our ranches and our house on San Francisco Street on the pretext that there were too many Cristeros in the family. On top of that, my father—who, despite his degree in engineering, was held in contempt for being the son of a tailor—squandered the inheritance from his father-in-law on one absurd business venture after another, like trying to set up an air route between cities in the interior of the country or exporting tequila to the United States. Then, using money borrowed from my maternal uncles, he bought the soap factory that did well during the war and then went under when the North American companies invaded the domestic market.

And that's why my mother never tired of repeating: We've ended up in this accursed Mexico City. Infamous place, Sodom and Gomorrah awaiting the fire rain, a hell where horrors, the likes of which were never seen in Guadalajara, like the crime I had just committed, were daily occurrences. Sinister Capital City where we had to live among the worst elements. Contagion, bad examples. Birds of a feather flock together. How could it be, she insisted again and again, that a supposedly *decent* school would accept a bastard (what's a bastard?), the illegitimate son of a kept woman? Because there really is no way of kowing who the father is when you consider how many clients that prostitute must have, that corrupter of youth. (What does that mean, an illegitimate son? What's a kept woman? Why do you call her a prostitute?)

My mother had momentarily forgotten all about Hector. Hector boasted about being the *stud* of the university. It was rumored that he was one of the right-wing militants who forced Zubirán, the rector, to resign and erased the sign that read "God does not exist" on the mural Diego Rivera painted in the Prado Hotel. Hector read *Mein Kampf,* books about Field Marshal Rommel, *A Brief History of Mexico* by Vasconcelos, *The Stallion in the Harem, Insatiable Nights, Memoirs of a Nymphomaniac,* pornographic novels published in Havana and sold under the counter on San Juan de Letrán and around Tívoli. My father devoured *How to Win Friends and Influence People, Achieving Self-Control, The Power of Positive Thinking, Life Begins at Forty.* My mother listened to all the radio soap operas on station XEW while she did her household chores, and sometimes she read something by Hugo Wast or M. Delly, to relax.

And to see Hector now! What a lean, bald, solemn, elegant fifty-year-old man my brother has become. So serious, grave, devout, respectable, so dignified in his role as a businessman at the service of the multinationals. A Catholic gentleman, the father of eleven children, an important member of the Mexican extreme right (in this respect, at least, he has always been impeccably coherent).

But in those remote days: the servants who took flight because "the young boss" would try to rape them (egged on by his gang's motto: "Make it with a maid," he would burst into their room on the roof at midnight, naked, erect, and impassioned by his novels; he would struggle with the girls and ejaculate on their nightgowns before managing to penetrate them, and then the shouts would awaken my parents; they would get up; my sisters and I would watch everything, our mouths hanging open, from the bottom of the winding stairway; they would scold Hector, threaten to throw him out of the house, and at that hour of the night would even fire the servant, an even guiltier party than "the young boss" for going around *leading him on*); venereal diseases contracted from Meave whores or those on Dos de Abril Street; a fight between two rival bands on the banks of the Piety River, one stone's throw that broke his incisors; a locksmith's skull cracked open with a rubber pipe; a visit to the police station because Hector and a bunch of friends from Urueta Park had taken some drugs and ransacked a cafeteria owned by a Chinese couple; my father having to pay the fine and the damages and pull strings in the government so they wouldn't send Hector to Lecumberri. When I heard Hector had taken drugs, I thought he owed some money because in my house debts were always referred to as drugs (as far as that goes, my father was the perfect drug addict). Later, Isabel, my older sister, explained to me what it was all about. It was only natural for Hector to be on my side: I had, at least provisionally, replaced him as the black sheep in the family.

XI ◦§ Specters

There was another uproar at the beginning of the year when Esteban became Isabel's boyfriend. In the 1930s, Esteban had been a famous child actor. Logically, when he grew up, he lost his sweet little voice and innocent face. They no longer gave him parts in movies or theater; he made a living reading jokes on Station XEW, drank like a fish, and was determined to marry Isabel and go to Hollywood to try his luck despite the fact that he did not speak a word of English. Whenever he came to see her, he was in a stupor and reeking of booze, without a tie, his suit stained and wrinkled, and wearing dirty shoes.

Nobody could figure it out. But Isabel was his devoted fan. In the absence of Tyrone Power, Errol Flynn, Clark Gable, Robert Mitchum, and Cary Grant, Esteban was Isabel's only chance of kiss-

ing a movie star, even if he did only star in the same Mexican
movies that had become the butt of family jokes at least as fre-
quently as Miguel Alemán's regime. Did you see Pedro Infante's
face? He looks just like a chauffeur. No wonder all the housemaids
are in love with him.

One night my father threw Esteban out of the house: he arrived
home late from English class and found him in the living room with
the lights dimmed and his hand up Isabel's skirt. Hector tossed him
out into the street, knocked him down, and then kept kicking him
until Esteban managed to get on his feet, all bloody, and run away
like a dog. Isabel refused to speak to Hector and began attacking
me at the slightest provocation, even though I had tried to stop my
brother from kicking poor Esteban on the ground. Isabel and Esteban
never saw each other again: a short time later, defeated by failure,
poverty, and alcoholism, he hanged himself in an infamous hotel in
Tacubaya. Sometimes they show his movies on television and I feel
like I am watching a ghost.

The only positive outcome of that period was that I got to have
my own room. Up until then, I had slept in twin beds with Estelita,
my little sister. Once I was diagnosed as a pervert, however, my
mother thought the girl might be in danger. They moved her into
the room with the older girls, much to the dismay of Isabel, who
was studying in a junior college, and Rosa Maria, who had just
gotten her diploma as an English-Spanish bilingual secretary.

Hector wanted to share my room with me. My parents refused.
In the aftermath of his most recent adventures with the police and
his latest attempts to rape the maid, Hector slept in the basement
under lock and key. He had only a few blankets and an old mat-
tress. My father used his old bedroom to store the factory's secret
accounts and repeat each lesson from his records a thousand times:
At what time did you go to bed last night, that you are not yet up?

*I went to bed very late, and I overslept myself. I could not sleep
until four o'clock in the morning. My servant did not call me,
therefore I did not wake up.* I don't know of any other adult who
learned to speak English in less than a year. Clearly, he had no other
choice.

Once, without them knowing, I overheard a conversation between
my parents. Poor little Carlos. Don't worry, he'll get over it. No,
this is going to have an adverse effect on his entire life. What bad
luck! How could this have happened to our son? We should think
of it as an accident, as if he had been hit by a truck or something,
don't you think? Within a few weeks, he won't even remember. If
he thinks we have been unfair to him now, he will realize, when he
grows up, that it was for his own good. It is all because of the immorality you breathe in this country with this corrupt government:
it's the worst we've ever had. Look at the magazines, the radio, the
movies: everything is part of a conspiracy to corrupt the innocent.

So, as it turned out, nobody could help me. I was completely
alone. Hector saw it all as a mischievous prank, something amus-
ing, like breaking a window with a ball. Neither my father nor my
brothers nor Mondragón nor Father Ferrán nor the authors of those
tests understood anything at all. They were judging me by standards
to which my behavior could not conform.

I began the second new school at the end of July. I knew nobody.
Once again I was the foreign intruder. There were no Jews or
Arabs, no poor kids on scholarships, no battles in the desert, although there was, as usual, mandatory English. The first few weeks
were hell. I could not stop thinking about Mariana. My parents
thought the punishments, the confession, the psychological tests—
the results of which I never saw—had cured me. Nevertheless, on
the sly and to the great surprise of the newspaper vendor, I bought
Vea and *Vodevil* and played with myself without bringing on

an ejaculation. Mariana's image reappeared, above and beyond Tongolele, Kalantán, Su Muy Key. No, I had not been cured: love is a disease in a world where the only natural thing is hatred.

I never saw Jim again. I never dared go near his house or back to the old school. When I thought of Mariana, the impulse to go see her was mixed with a sensation of discomfort and ridicule. How stupid of me to have gotten involved in such a mess that could have been avoided by simply repressing my idiotic declaration of love. Too late for regrets: I did what I had to do, and even now, so many years later, I cannot deny that I had fallen in love with Mariana.

XII ᴥ§ The Roman Quarter

There was a big earthquake in October. A comet appeared in November. It was said that these presaged an atomic war, the end of the world or, at the very least, another revolution in Mexico. Then La Sirena Hardware Store burned down, and many people were killed. By the time Christmas vacation came around, everything had totally changed for us. My father had sold his soap factory and had just been appointed manager of the North American company that had bought him out. Hector was studying at the University of Chicago, and my older sisters were in Texas.

One day at noon I was returning home after playing tennis at the Junior Club. I was seated sideways on a bus on the Santa María line reading a Perry Mason novel when, on the corner of Insurgentes and Álvaro Obregón, Rosales boarded the bus and asked the driver for permission to sell the Adams Chewing Gum he was carrying in a small box. He saw me. Ashamed, he jumped off the bus as fast as he could and hid behind a tree near Alfonso y Marcos, where my mother used to get her permanents and manicures before she had her own car and could go to a salon in Polanco.

Rosales: the poorest boy in my old school, whose mother was an orderly in a hospital. Everything happened in a matter of seconds. I jumped off the Santa María while it was in motion; Rosales tried to escape; I caught up with him. Ridiculous scene: Rosales, please don't be ashamed. It's great that you're working (look at me, who'd never worked a day in his life). You shouldn't be ashamed of helping your mother (look at me, playing the role of *Doctor Lovesick from Her Soul Clinic*). Hey, come on, I'll buy you an ice cream at La Bella Italia. You can't imagine how happy I am to see you (look at me being magnanimous with money to spare, in spite of devaluation and inflation). Rosales: sullen, pale, retreating. Finally he stopped and looked me in the eyes.

No, Carlitos, I would rather you bought me a sandwich, if you don't mind. I haven't eaten breakfast. I'm really starving. Listen, aren't you still mad at me because of our fights? What are you talking about Rosales? Those fights don't matter now (look at me, the generous one, capable of forgiving because I had become invulnerable). Okay, Carlitos, let's sit down and talk.

We crossed Obregón, then Insurgentes. So, tell me: did you get through the school year? How did Jim do on his exams? What did they all say when I never returned to school? Rosales kept quiet. We sat down in a sandwich shop. He ordered one sausage and two steak sandwiches and a soda. And you, Carlitos, aren't you going to eat? I can't: they're expecting me at home. Today my mother made roast beef, my favorite. If I eat anything now, I won't be able to eat later. Just bring me a Coke and make it very cold.

Rosales put the box of Adams on the table. He looked out onto Insurgentes: the Packards, Buicks, Hudsons, the yellow streetcars, silver-colored lampposts, multicolored buses, the pedestrians who were still wearing hats: a scene and a moment that will never be repeated. The building in front: General Electric, Helvex Heaters, Mabe Stoves. A long silence; mutual discomfort. Rosales very restless, avoiding my eyes. He wiped his damp hands on his worn-out tweed pants.

They brought the food. Rosales took a bite out of the sausage sandwich. Before chewing it, he took a sip of water to wet it down. It was nauseating. Drawn-out hunger and anxiety: he devoured it. He asked me with his mouth full: And you? Did you get through the year even with the change of school? Are you going somewhere for vacation? On the jukebox, "La Múcura" ended and "Ghost Riders in the Sky" began. We are going to meet my brothers and sisters in New York for Christmas. We already have reservations at the Plaza Hotel. Do you know what the Plaza is? But listen, why don't you answer my questions?

Rosales swallowed saliva, sandwich, and soda. I thought he was going to choke. Well, Carlitos, it is just that, look, I don't know how to tell you this. Everybody in our class knew everything. What's everything? That thing about his mother. Jim told every single one of us. *He hates you.* We all thought that what you did was pretty funny. You're really nuts. And to top it off, someone saw you confessing in church after your declaration of love. And some- how word got out that they had taken you to the nut house.

I didn't respond. Rosales kept eating in silence. Suddenly he lifted his eyes and looked at me: I didn't want to tell you, Carlitos, but that isn't the worst part. No, someone else should tell you. Let me finish my sandwiches. They're delicious. I haven't eaten for a whole day. My mother lost her job at the hospital because she was trying to organize a union. And the guy who lives with her now says that since I'm not his son, he has no obligation to support me. Rosales, really, I'm sorry to hear that, but it's none of my business and I have no reason to get involved. Eat whatever you want and however much you want—I'm paying—but tell me the worst part.

Well, okay, Carlitos, it's just that it makes me real sad, you have no idea. Out with it, Rosales, once and for all, don't play around with me. It's just that, look Carlitos, I don't know how to tell you: Jim's mother is dead. Dead? What do you mean, dead? Yes, yes, Jim isn't at school anymore. In October he went to live in San Francisco. His real father came and got him. It was horrible. You have no idea. It seems like she had some kind of argument or something with that Señor who Jim said was his father but wasn't. He and his mother—her name was Mariana, right?—were in a caberet or a restaurant or a very elegant party in Las Lomas. They were arguing about something she had said about the thieves in the government, about how they squandered the money they stole from the poor. The Señor didn't like that, and he raised his voice in front of all his powerful friends: ministers, foreign millionaires, his top associates in all his business schemes, whatever. And he slapped her right there in front of everybody, and he screamed at her that she had no right to talk about honor because she was a whore. Mariana got up and went home in a taxi and took a bottle of Nembutal and slit her wrists with a razor blade and shot herself, and she did all of it at once, I'm not sure how it was exactly. Anyway, Jim woke up and found her dead, lying in a pool of blood. He almost died too from pain and fear. And since the doorman of the building wasn't there, Jim went to Mondragón: he had nowhere else to turn. You should have seen the crowds of curious onlookers and the Green Cross and the agent from the public prosecutor's office and the police. I didn't dare look at her dead, but when they brought her out on the cot the sheets were covered with blood. For all of us, it was the worst thing that had ever happened to us in our lives. She left Jim a letter in English, a long letter asking him to forgive her and explaining to him everything I just told you. I think she also left some other notes—maybe there was even one for you, but there'd be no way of finding out—but they disappeared because the Señor covered everything up immediately, and they forbade us to talk about it among ourselves and especially at home. But you know how gossip flies and how difficult it is to keep a secret. Poor Jim, poor old buddy, how much we teased him at school! I really feel bad about it.

Rosales, this isn't possible. You're pulling my leg. You invented everything you just told me. You saw it in some fucking Mexican movie, the kind you like. You heard it on some sleazy soap opera on station XEW. Those things can't happen. Don't joke with me like that, please.

It's true, Carlitos. I swear to God it's true. May my mother drop dead if I told a lie. Ask anyone you want to at school. Talk to Mondragón. Everyone knows, even though it didn't come out in the papers. I'm surprised you didn't find out about it until now. Remember, I didn't want to be the one to tell you: that's why I hid, not because of the chewing gum. Carlitos, don't look at me like that: are you crying? I know, it's really terrible and horrible what happened. I was also very upset by it, you have no idea. But you're not going to tell me that seriously, at your age, you were in love with Jim's mom.

Instead of answering, I got up, paid with a ten-peso bill, and walked out without even waiting for the change or saying good-bye. I saw death everywhere: in the little pieces of animal about to become sandwiches and tacos, along with the onions, tomatoes, lettuce, cheese, cream, beans, guacamole, jalapeño peppers. Live animals like the trees they had just finished pruning on Insurgentes. I saw death in the soft drinks: Mission Orange, Spur, Ferroquina; in the cigarettes: Belmont, Gratos, Elegantes, Casinos.

I ran down Tabasco Street telling myself, trying to tell myself: It's one of Rosales's bluffs, an idiotic joke, he has always been a jerk. He wanted to get his revenge because I saw him starving to death with his little box of chewing gum and me with my tennis racket, my white suit, my Perry Mason in English, my reservations at the Plaza. I don't care if Jim opens the door. I don't care if I make a fool of myself. Even though everyone is going to laugh at me, I want to see Mariana. I want to prove that Mariana isn't dead.

I arrived at the building, dried my tears with a Kleenex, walked up the stairs, rang the doorbell to Apartment 4. A girl about fifteen years old answered the door. Mariana? No, no one by the name of Mariana lives here. This is the home of the Morales family. We moved here two months ago. I don't know who might have lived here before. Maybe you should ask the doorman.

While the girl was talking, I looked past her into a different living room: dirty, poor, disorderly. No pictures of Mariana at Semo's or of Jim at the Golden Gate Bridge or of the *Señor serving his country* with the president's team. Instead of all that, the Last Supper in metallic relief and a calendar with pictures from The Legend of the Volcanoes.

The doorman in the building was also new. The one from before wasn't there anymore: Don Sindulfo, Zapata's old ex-colonel who had become Jim's friend and sometimes told us stories about the Revolution and cleaned the apartment because Mariana didn't like having maids. No, son, I don't know any Don Sindulfo or this Jim you're talking about. There's no Mariana here. Forget it kid, don't insist. I offered him twenty pesos. Not even if you give me a thousand, kid. I can't accept it because I don't know nothing about nothing.

Nevertheless, he did take the money and let me carry on my search. At that moment I remembered that the building belonged to the Señor, and he had hired Don Sindulfo because his father— who Jim called "my grandpa"—had been a friend of the old man when they had both fought in the Revolution. I rang all the doorbells. I was so ridiculous with my little white tennis suit and my racket and my Perry Mason, asking questions, my face on the verge of tears peering in through the door. The smell of rice soup, the smell of chiles rellenos. In all the apartments they listened to me almost fearfully. My white suit was so incongruent! This was the house of death, not a tennis court.

No. I've been in this building since 1939 and as far as I know, no one by the name of Mariana has ever lived here. Jim? Don't know him either. In Apartment 8 there is a kid about your age named Everardo. In Apartment 4? No, an old couple without children lived there. But I came over here to Jim and Mariana's house a million times. You're imagining things, kid. It must have been on another street, in another building. Okay, good-bye. Don't waste any more of my time. Don't get involved in what's none of your business and create more problems. Enough kid, please. I have to get lunch ready; my husband gets home at two-thirty. But, ma'am. Go away or I'll call the police, and they'll take you straight to the juvenile authorities.

I returned home and I can't remember what I did afterward. I must have cried for days. Then we went to New York, I stayed at a school in Virginia. I remember, I don't remember even what year it was. Just these bursts, these flashes of light that bring everything back and the exact words. Just that little song that I will never hear again: "However high the heavens or the skies, / however deep the ocean lies."

How ancient! How remote! What an impossible story! But Mariana existed; Jim existed; everything I went over in my head existed even after such a long time of refusing to confront it. I will never know if the suicide really happened. I never again saw Rosales or anybody else from that period. They demolished the school; they demolished Mariana's building; they demolished my house; they demolished the Roman Quarter. That city came to an end. That country was finished. There is no memory of the Mexico of those years. And nobody cares: who could feel nostalgic for that horror? Everything came to an end just like the records on the jukebox. I will never know if Mariana is still alive. If she is, she would be sixty years old.

New Directions Paperbooks—A Partial Listing

For complete listing request free catalog from
New Directons, 80 Eighth Avenue, New York 10011   † Bilingual

From Your Capricorn Friend. NDP568.
  The Smile at the Foot of the Ladder. NDP386.
  Stand Still Like the Hummingbird. NDP236.
  The Time of the Assassins. NDP115.
Y. Mishima, Confessions of a Mask. NDP253.
  Death in Midsummer. NDP215.
Mistral, Frédéric, The Memoirs. NDP632.
Eugenio Montale, It Depends.† NDP507.
  New Poems. NDP410.
  Selected Poems.† NDP193.
Paul Morand, Fancy Goods/Open All Night.
  NDP567.
Vladimir Nabokov, Nikolai Gogol. NDP78.
  Laughter in the Dark. NDP470.
  The Real Life of Sebastian Knight. NDP432.
P. Neruda, The Captain's Verses.† NDP345.
  Residence on Earth.† NDP340.
New Directions in Prose & Poetry (Anthology).
  Available from #17 forward; #50, Fall 1986.
Robert Nichols, Arrival. NDP437.
  Exile. NDP485. Garh City. NDP450.
  Harditts in Sawna. NDP470.
Charles Olson, Selected Writings. NDP231.
Toby Olson, The Life of Jesus. NDP417.
  Seaview. NDP532.
  We Are the Fire. NDP580.
George Oppen, Collected Poems. NDP418.
István Örkeny, The Flower Show /
  The Toth Family. NDP536.
Wilfred Owen, Collected Poems. NDP210.
Nicanor Parra, Antipoems: New & Selected. NDP603.
Boris Pasternak, Safe Conduct. NDP77.
Kenneth Patchen, Aflame and Afun. NDP292.
  Because It Is. NDP83.
  But Even So. NDP265.
  Collected Poems. NDP284.
  Hallelujah Anyway. NDP219.
  Selected Poems. NDP160.
Octavio Paz, Configurations.† NDP303.
  A Draft of Shadows.† NDP489.
  Eagle or Sun?† NDP422.
  Selected Poems. NDP574.
St. John Perse.† Selected Poems. NDP545.
Plays for a New Theater (Anth.) NDP216.
J. A. Porter, Eelgrass. NDP438.
Ezra Pound, ABC of Reading. NDP89.
  Confucius. NDP285.
  Confucius to Cummings. (Anth.) NDP126.
  Gaudier Brzeska. NDP372.
  Guide to Kulchur. NDP257.
  Literary Essays. NDP250.
  Selected Cantos. NDP304.
  Selected Letters 1907-1941. NDP317.
  Selected Poems. NDP66.
  The Spirit of Romance. NDP266.
  Translations.† (Enlarged Edition) NDP145.
  Women of Trachis. NDP597.
Raymond Queneau, The Bark Tree. NDP314.
  The Blue Flowers. NDP595.
  Exercises in Style. NDP513.
  The Sunday of Life. NDP433.
Mary de Rachewiltz, Ezra Pound. NDP405.
Raja Rao, Kanthapura. NDP224.
Herbert Read, The Green Child. NDP208.
P. Reverdy, Selected Poems.† NDP346.
Kenneth Rexroth, Classics Revisited. NDP621.
  100 More Poems from the Chinese. NDP308.
  100 More Poems from the Japanese.† NDP420.
  100 Poems from the Chinese. NDP192.
  100 Poems from the Japanese.† NDP147.
  Selected Poems. NDP581.
  Women Poets of China. NDP528.
  Women Poets of Japan. NDP527.
Rainer Maria Rilke, Poems from
  The Book of Hours. NDP408.
  Possibility of Being. (Poems). NDP436.
  Whee Silence Reigns. (Prose). NDP464.
Arthur Rimbaud, Illuminations.† NDP56.
  Season in Hell & Drunken Boat.† NDP97.
Edouard Roditi, Delights of Turkey. NDP445.

Oscar Wilde. NDP624.
Jerome Rothenberg, That Dada Strain. NDP550.
  New Selected Poems. NDP625.
Saigyo,† Mirror for the Moon. NDP465.
Saikaku Ihara, The Life of an Amorous
  Woman. NDP270.
St. John of the Cross, Poems.† NDP341.
Jean-Paul Sartre, Nausea. NDP82.
  The Wall (Intimacy). NDP272.
Delmore Schwartz, Selected Poems. NDP241.
  In Dreams Begin Responsibilities. NDP454.
Stevie Smith, Collected Poems. NDP562.
Gary Snyder, The Back Country. NDP249.
  The Real Work. NDP499.
  Regarding Wave. NDP306.
  Turtle Island. NDP381.
Enid Starkie, Rimbaud. NDP254.
Robert Steiner, Bathers. NDP495.
Jules Supervielle, Selected Writings.† NDP209.
Tabucchi, Antonio, Letter from Casablanca. NDP620.
Nathaniel Tarn, Lyrics . . . Bride of God. NDP391.
Dylan Thomas, Adventures in the Skin Trade.
  NDP183.
  A Child's Christmas in Wales. NDP181.
  Collected Poems 1934-1952. NDP316.
  Collected Stories. NDP626.
  Portrait of the Artist as a Young Dog. NDP51.
  Quite Early One Morning. NDP90.
  Under Milk Wood. NDP73.
Tian Wen: A Chinese Book of Origins. NDP624.
Lionel Trilling, E. M. Forster. NDP189.
Martin Turnell, Baudelaire. NDP336.
  Rise of the French Novel. NDP474.
Paul Valéry, Selected Writings.† NDP184.
Elio Vittorini, A Vittorini Omnibus. NDP366.
Robert Penn Warren, At Heaven's Gate. NDP588.
Vernon Watkins, Selected Poems. NDP221.
Weinberger, Eliot, Works on Paper. NDP627.
Nathanael West, Miss Lonelyhearts &
  Day of the Locust. NDP125.
J. Wheelwright, Collected Poems. NDP544.
J. Williams. An Ear in Bartram's Tree. NDP335.
Tennessee Williams, Camino Real. NDP301.
  Cat on a Hot Tin Roof. NDP398.
  Clothes for a Summer Hotel. NDP556.
  The Glass Menagerie. NDP218.
  Hard Candy. NDP225.
  In the Winter of Cities. NDP154.
  A Lovely Sunday for Creve Coeur. NDP497.
  One Arm & Other Stories. NDP237.
  Stopped Rocking. NDP575.
  A Streetcar Named Desire. NDP501.
  Sweet Bird of Youth. NDP409.
  Twenty-Seven Wagons Full of Cotton. NDP217.
  Vieux Carre. NDP482.
William Carlos Williams,
  The Autobiography. NDP223.
  The Buildup. NDP259.
  The Doctor Stories. NDP585.
  I Wanted to Write a Poem. NDP469.
  Imaginations. NDP329.
  In the American Grain. NDP53.
  In the Money. NDP240.
  Paterson. Complete. NDP152.
  Pictures form Brueghel. NDP118.
  Selected Letters. NDP589.
  Selected Poems (new ed.). NDP602.
  White Mule. NDP226.
  Yes, Mrs. Williams. NDP534.
Yvor Winters, E. A. Robinson. NDP326.
Wisdom Books: Ancient Egyptians.NDP467.
  Early Buddhists, NDP444; English Mystics.
  NDP466; Forest (Hindu). NDP414; Spanish
  Mystics. NDP442; St. Francis. NDP477;
  Sufi. NDP424; Taoists. NDP509; Wisdom of
  the Desert. NDP295; Zen Masters. NDP415.

Made in the USA
Lexington, KY
27 April 2011